The Edge of the World

Gail Vida Hamburg

Miráre Press

No part of this book may be used or reproduced in any manner without written permission of the author, except for brief quotations used in reviews and critiques.

This book is a work of fiction. Names, characters, settings and incidents are either the product of the author's imagination or used fictitiously. Any resemblance to actual events, settings or persons, living or dead, is entirely coincidental.

Printed in the United States of America

Published by Miráre Press, Boston, MA

ISBN 978-0-9798275-9-4

First edition 2007

Library of Congress Control Number 2007935670

For more information, please contact Miráre Press at (617)-314-6856 or e-mail information@mirarepress.com

Author's Note

The Quiet American, Graham Greene's prophetic novel about American foreign policy in Vietnam, was a source of inspiration to me during the writing of this book. I have been moved to reference it, as a historical marker and literary device, in this fiction. A familiarity with Greene's novel will greatly enhance an understanding of mine.

GVH

Acknowledgments

I am grateful to my teachers at Bennington Writing Seminars: Askold Melnyczuk, Alice Mattison, Sheila Kohler, and Martha Cooley for their guidance during the writing of this book. Thanks are not enough.

Thanks to agents Robin Strauss and Fiona Hallowell for their efforts on behalf of this work from 2005 to 2007.

Orchids to Vanina Marsot, Shanti Thyil, Gary Wolfe, Ethelbert Miller, and Joan Digby for reading early drafts and revisions, and Georgina Gomez for daily fellowship.

Thanks to Chandan Crasta & David Collins and team for book art and science.

I thank my family—Charles and Joshua Hamburg, Vitus and Rodrigo Silva—for ballast, space, and wings.

For my father, Peter Tom Silva.

The Edge of the World

Gail Vida Hamburg

I am the place in which something has occurred.
—Claude Levi-Strauss

Contents

Some Enchanted Island

(1950s – 1960s)

Presidential Visit

Everything American came to Chomumbhar, my sleepy sleeping island on the Indian Ocean—latitude 28 degrees south, longitude 78 degrees east—after JFK and Jackie. In villas, bungalows, and attap houses across the archipelago, glossy pictures of the couple, neatly excised from *Life* magazine, looked down from altars and prayer walls. In my family's living room, a framed photograph of the President and his wife leaned splay-legged on a rosewood chiffonier, next to a Pietà cast in marble and an alabaster statue of Francis Xavier, patron saint of the East Indies.

One July morning in 1962, Muni, our eleven-year-old house girl, hurried home from market. Our house was the first in a crescent of twenty villas in a secluded Christian enclave on Tilika Heights, a promontory overlooking Resurrection Beach and the Indian Ocean. From the tall windows in the living room, and the deck of *mangaris* redwood that hugged the facade, we could watch the sea change its face by the hour. Serene teal just before dawn, flushed vermilion at sunrise, fluttering emerald after breakfast, angry moss green at high tide, tired ebony at dusk. And above it, a dome, a particular daily sky of a specific blueness—azure, cerulean, cobalt, sapphire, turquoise. Squinting into the distance, you could see water and sky held together by a barely discernible thread of pale silk.

I was an only child, raised in a household of praying women, neglected by a father who had surrendered his life to politics and nation building, and educated by nuns. The sea, solitude, and religion turned me into a pensive young girl. When I was not quite seven, I thought the earth stopped where

I could will my gaze no further, that the ocean flowed over the rim like water from the lip of a tub when you sank heavily into it. Though that worried me at first, I consoled myself that on the other side, farther than my eye could see, there must have been a girl just like me, alone but not lonely, playing with her dolls, eating mangosteens, going to school, doing homework, praying in church, and being loved.

So much of the time, life seemed long and ordinary. When I wanted my heart to lurch with excitement and fear, I would raid the pantry for bread, as many slices as I could fit into the cradle of my arms, and slowly descend the stairway at the side of our house leading to the beach. I would stand at the water's edge and fling slice after slice of the bread, as far as I could into the water. Sometimes, I would hurl the bread with such force, it felt like my shoulder was being wrenched out of its socket. The sky above would turn dark quickly, as birds from everywhere appeared and formed a dark canopy. There would be a sound, a whirr, as thousands of wings flapped to keep the birds aloft. And then, as I stopped tossing the bread, to offer my arm some relief, they would swoop down en masse and fight for the slices. I would watch them racing to the water, gliding and riding the winds without exerting themselves, dropping down to pick what they could before soaring higher and higher still. I would walk into the water until it reached my ankles, and throw the bread into the water until there was no more left, and the birds had disappeared. The lake would turn to inky blue as the sun gradually drowned in it. Sometimes I heard a *raga* rising from under the waves, a yearning flute that leached its way under my skin and asserted itself in the liquid, soft places.

Long before my emotions could be formed into a shape that I could seriously hold, a feeling came over me that was different from every other feeling I had ever had. It did not float away like a dawn hallucination, but dropped down my throat and glommed onto the wall of my chest. Slowly, during the course of a monsoon season the year I turned nine, as I watched the impenetrable drama outside the windows that would not yield itself to me, as I watched the arrival and departure of contingents of arctic tern, sula sula, and frigates, I discerned an essential thing about myself. I divined, in some inexplicable way, that unlike the terns who flew around the world several times each year, I belonged to that place and nowhere else, that I would never venture far from home, that I would live, grow old, and die on the island.

Muni had been running errands for my mother at Change Alley, the bustling central market in town. The Alley-*Aleia Mudanca* was a legacy of the island's Portuguese colonizers. A popular shopping and dining bazaar in Port Contadu, it had been built in the manner of town squares in Lisbon. An ornate archway of marble and majolica framed a central square, which was ringed by three colossal lime-washed *palacios*. The buildings had ochre facades, red roofs, overhead balconies, and verandas below. The square in the center, *Largo Dourado*— Golden Square, was paved with gold leaf tiles. A statue of Saint Francis Xavier rose from a red stone podium in the middle of the square. The bearded life-sized figure wearing the brown robes of the Jesuits had sharp Caucasian features and the honey-tinged complexion of most islanders. His right arm and the brown sleeve covering it ended above the elbow.

On the paved walkways ringing the *palacios*, vendors with peddler licenses plied their wares from baskets and boxes. They offered small assortments of pastries, sweets, handmade jewelry, eggs, and flowers. My mother never bought from them. She complained that they offered slim pickings, moved their trading posts by the hour, and took off at the first sighting of storm clouds. Mama preferred the fully established merchants under the portico, who offered abundant selections of groceries, produce, and flowers. She also frequented the stalls and restaurants in the arcade, where skilled cooks offered all manner of prepared delicacies and desserts. At the large emporiums and expensive boutiques on both sides of the arches, Sindhi businesses with names like Lal and Doshi sold fine clothing, precious gems and jewelry, oriental rugs, and antiques. Cars were restricted from the plaza and its vicinity, although Daud, our family's chauffeur, routinely drove our sedan with its white PON (Persons of Note) license plates through the arched entryway to *Largo Dourado.* "I won't be long," Mama would say, waving her bangled hand at Daud and me before she ambled over to the stalls to look for just the right stems of blush pink Gelinta highland roses, trumpet-shaped orange hibiscus, and rare orchids—Elephant Ear, Catherine's Slipper, Isabella's Ring, Jewel Tongue. She prayed hard and often to Saint Francis to compensate for my father's mortal and venial sins, and hoped to gain the Saint's favor with pins and expensive bouquets.

Muni's skirt flapped around her ankles, and her oiled braid swung like a pendulum, from the morning breeze and her own whirlwind. She walked urgently to the house, hugging a large straw bag sprouting long beans and lady's fingers. The tight sleeves of her blouse were so long they ended where her fingers began.

"Mem, Mem, the sun has shined up my alley! Hurry, open the gate. News! I have news!" Muni shrieked, rattling the latch of the wrought iron gates in front of our house. "It's too much to bear!" she cried.

"Who died?" My mother asked, emerging from the house and onto the verandah, one hand on her hip, the other drawing a key from a black cord fastened to a loop on her sarong. The key was her weapon, her defense against beggars, hawkers, and other intruders who dared to venture to the Heights.

The last time the entrance had been left unlocked, Muni and her mother had walked into our lives. My mother ordered keys for herself a few days later. At first, she tied the key to a rubber band and looped it around her wrist. Later, she threaded the key with cords of increasing elegance (silks, velvets, brocades) that complemented the colors of her clothes, and attached them to the waist of her sarongs.

Save for that stubborn attention to pragmatism, my mother, the sentinel, lived in her own alternate, paradoxical reality—a world of delicate Portuguese poetry, steamy Hindi films, and heroic Catholic martyrs and saints. She read aloud the poems of Cesare Verde and Fernando Pessoa to my father and I, while we ate breakfast. She told me that watching Bombay musicals— Night in London, Evening in Paris, and Love in Tokyo—made the sun less harsh and the rain go away. She often said that if she hadn't married, she would have been a mystic. When she wanted something desperately, something beyond her reach that could not be bought with my father's influence or money, she prayed for it. If it was a miracle she desired, my mother would petition Saint Francis and the Madonna by piercing her thigh with a Miraculous Medal lapel pin. She would thread the pin through her skin, lock it in place, and leave it there until her prayer was answered. Most of the women we knew performed penance of some sort or other. Some wore only white clothes, others no makeup, some rejected jewelry, others lived as married celibates, some wore their hair cropped like Joan of Arc, others wore veils, some ate only unsalted food, and others bread and water. Mama told me she had received innumerable graces throughout her life because of her mortification. Once, she took my forefinger and traced a circle around the medal lodged in her thigh. "Sometimes, you have to dare God," she said. I was not a delicate child, but her recklessness frightened me.

In 1540, the King of Portugal sent Francis Xavier and his Society of Jesus to evangelize the East. It was so ambitious a mission, the King called it the church that would spring from the wound in Christ's side. The Brown Robes made their way first to Goa, then Moluccus, Amboine, and Malacca. At each port, they preached and stayed long enough to hold mass water baptisms in the sea. The natives, as many as ten thousand at a time, were promised heaven, led into the water, and given a new faith. After the final blessings, the Jesuits would hand each convert a paper bearing their new name: Santiago Almadovar, Fatima Gomez, Franco Fernandez, Isabella D'Silva, Lucia Lopez.

Francis Xavier and his Jesuits set sail for Chomumbhar in 1545. According to local legend, their ship was caught in a furious storm before reaching the island, and only Xavier's prayers quelled the fury. Grateful for the boat's safe landing, Xavier thanked God and blessed the crabs. We believe in this story because it is the only explanation we have for the Missionary crabs. Chomumbhar and Malacca are the only two places in the world where crabs have crosses on their backs— crucifixes engraved on their shells. Whenever our fishermen caught Missionary crabs in their nets, they were bound by their faith to toss them back into the sea. We do not eat Missionary crabs, out of respect for God and Saint Francis Xavier. The islanders began to call the stretch of white beach where the Brown Robes landed, Resurrection Beach.

As for the saint, he traveled to many other places in Asia after Chomumbhar. He sailed to Japan and Macau, and finally to China, where he died in 1552. His body is enshrined in a glass coffin in Goa, but his right arm was severed and taken to Rome. The arm lies in a glass reliquary in the Church of Gesù, brown and scaly in death, but still adamant, the fingers spread in a supplication—come to me, follow me.

"President is coming! Mem Jackie coming too!" Muni said.

"Here? To the edge of the world? I don't believe it," Mama

said, releasing the squat lock and opening the gate. Cradled by the Indian Ocean and surrounded by four continents, Chomumbhar dipped close to the bottom of the globe. Nothing ever happened there, we were sure of it. "What have I told you about bluffing?" Mama twisted Muni's ear.

"I'm not bluffing. People at the market say so." Muni cupped both her ears to protect them. "On the bus too, people said so. Listen to radio."

I ran to the living room and turned on the radio, a mahogany bureau with an emblem of a dog shouting into a megaphone. Radio Chomumbhar, the only station on the dial, was in the middle of Breakfast in Paradise—a daily variety show featuring local news, classical music, and government edicts on how to behave. The rules and regulations were essential elements of Prime Minister Ferdinand D'Souza's 20/20 Vision Plan, and violating them resulted in fines and penalties.

- Littering – 500 *flores*
- Spitting in public – 750 *flores*
- Urinating in public places – 1500 *flores*
- Fraternizing with Qalit (Untouchables) – fine of 5000 *flores* and ten lashes of bamboo cane.
- Intimate relations with Qalit – same as above and imprisonment of up to five years.

I was twelve then, old enough to know the laws but not their transgressors.

"Turn it up," my mother said, her fingers curled around Muni's wrist.

A news bulletin soon followed. "Prime Minister Ferdinand D'Souza and Lady Lalitha are proud to announce the visit next month of President John F. Kennedy and First Lady Jacqueline to Chomumbhar," the DJ intoned in a grand manner.

The sun had shone up all our alleys!

The DJ interviewed my father, the Prime Minister's press secretary, by telephone.

"It will be in four weeks … August thirty first … a three day stopover on their way to India … It behooves us to work with alacrity … It is the Prime Minister's wish that Chomumbhar is represented sharply," Papa said.

Muni smiled, smug, as if she herself had arranged the visit.

"Four weeks. No time at all," my mother said.

"I told you I'm not bluffing," Muni said.

"You're innocent today," Mama agreed.

Muni was nine when her mother, Raji, brought her to us on a Sunday afternoon two years earlier. Mama was standing by the altar in the living room alcove, arranging flowers at the feet of Saint Francis. We had recently returned from Hole Comfort—the Cathedral of the Holy Comforter in Port Contadu, the capital—without my father.

The Prime Minister had summoned him as usual. Almost every Sunday, as Father Daniel Sullivan, our American parish priest, celebrated Mass, one of the PM's bodyguards would appear at the side door near the confessionals, hovering there until he caught my father's attention. When Father Daniel turned to face the tabernacle or parishioners began to form lines for Communion, my father would quickly dip his knee, cross himself, and slip out of the pew. The guard would drive my father to the Prime Minister's residence in Port Contadu or his retreat on Tilika Hill, or to Miramar, the PM's private golf course. After Mass, Daud would drive Mama and me, first to Change Alley, and then home. When I was younger, my mother used to complain directly to my father about his unholy exits.

"So disrespectful!" She would scold him in a whisper. "You put the PM before God?"

"Yes," my father would whisper back, before leaving.

"You must know my time is not my own," Papa often apologized, for ruining my mother's carefully laid plans for dinner and Sunday mass, christenings, weddings, funerals, and society.

Mama and I gradually learned not to expect too much from him. We allowed him to rest on the margins of our lives, and sought him out only when we needed him. "He takes good care of us," Mama would say, explaining away his absence at the events that marked our lives

"God flashed a picture of you in my mind when I prayed," Raji told my mother as Muni looked on.

My mother was clipping orchid stems with a pair of shears while holding the stalks in a bowl of water. She must have been flattered, for she did not shout for Daud.

Raji was a woman of thirty or so, with jaundiced eyes, cheeks that caved in, and breasts that collapsed. She dropped a knotted cloth bundle to the floor.

"My daughter can cook. Bake even." Raji adjusted the *paloo* of her sari that had slid down her shoulder.

"I have a cook and I enjoy baking." My mother arranged the flowers, casting her expert gaze over them, adjusting them to match some image in her head.

"Rich women should do other things," Raji said.

"Sita does everything," Mama replied.

Sita, our everything-doer, had been my grandmother's cook for years. Nenah sent Sita to my mother soon after my parents returned from their honeymoon. My father often joked that the only dowry he received from Nenah was a grumpy, betel-chewing Tamil woman with an affinity for toddy.

"Muni can do it when Sita don't like." Raji turned to her daughter. "Isn't that right, Muni?"

Muni shifted from one leg to another. She was wearing a smock, its frilly leg-of-mutton sleeves so long they grazed her knuckles.

"Just a baby." Mama pruned back a long, leafy stem as she eyed Muni. "Have you had your menses yet?"

Muni clung to her mother's waist.

"I have two sons to feed, nothing for her." Raji untangled herself from Muni's clasp.

"I eat enough," Muni said.

"Maybe in two or three years." Mama turned away.

"Show the lady." Raji's voice rose in a panic.

Muni remained where she stood.

"Show her." Raji pinched Muni. She slapped her across the arm and pushed her toward my mother.

Muni hung her head low as she stepped forward. She pushed both sleeves up to her elbows. She extended both hands to my mother—fists clenched, palm side down. Embossed on the slope of each hand before the fingers curled into their palms, were purple-brown spots, badly healed scars the size of plums.

My mother brought a hand to her throat. She was right to be nervous. While the Untouchable laws had been designed to keep the Qalit from offending the Rahmins, the natives of Chomumbhar—Lady Lalitha, wife of the Prime Minister, chief among them—everyone on the island was expected to obey them. A junior Labor minister, Christian like us, had narrowly escaped ten lashes for hiring a Qalit houseboy.

Raji and Muni did not look like Qalits; their complexions were pleasing—the color of milky tea—and their features were fine.

"You call us Untouchable," said Raji. "We call ourselves the Broken People."

Mama held Muni's hands in her own as she studied the marks. "What do they use?"

"Ask your husband," Raji said.

Since the 1500s, Chomumbhar had been colonized and conquered, conquered and colonized, first by the Portuguese, then the Dutch, and then the English. The Rahmins, the indigenous people, clung to their racial pride and identity by calling themselves "children of the soil." As dramatic new hybrids of islanders sprung from all the racial mixing, the Rahmins touted their superiority as the pure ones, with a multiplied ferocity. Bastardized islanders of every stripe, D'Souza and Valesco, Van Heusen and De Beer, and Cummings and Postlewaite, reinforced the Rahmins feelings of purity. The Qalit, ebony-skinned, coarse-haired descendants of locals and their unions with African traders, from Mozambique and Madagascar, offended the Rahmins the most. Lady Lalitha and several members of the Cabinet had a profound hatred for the Qalit and drafted laws to keep them in their place. The Prime Minister, who was not Rahmin but Catholic like us, enacted the laws to appease his wife. The race laws consigned the Qalit to the lowest rank of the caste system: they were officially referred to as Untouchables. Qalits were the island's street sweepers, garbage collectors, sewer workers, and gravediggers.

* * *

"Don't worry, little Muni," one of the two women who came for me said. They looked alike, wearing the same uniforms, and wearing their hair the same way, pulled back into buns. "It will all be over soon," the other woman smiled.

Both of them held me tight. I was not afraid of them or to go with them for I was bold, but I felt that I had to fight because of what I saw in my Ama's eyes. So I held on to my Ama, to every part of her—her body, her limbs, her clothes, her face, her hair. I put up a good fight, but I had to stop, not because the women were strong, but because my Ama was weak. She was crying from my pulling at her, so I had to give up. When the women saw that they had won, they bundled me into the van without any trouble. I could hear my Ama crying outside the van but I

13

could not see her. When I tried to wipe my tears, my hands felt gritty. I looked down at my hands and saw that my fists were filled with my Ama's hair.

The women took me to a building like a doctor's office. They waited with me until a man came. He was wearing a shining white coat and smiled so kindly, the way my Apa smiled when I woke from bad dreams. He carried a board with paper attached to it. "Have you had an injection before?" He led me down a corridor lined with many doors. He had nice grandfather's hair, all gray with just a little bit of black poking out on top.

"Three times already," I said, full of boast.

"Then this will be nothing." He smiled so wide, the skin on the side of his eyes made stripes. He opened one of the doors, and when I saw that it was a doctor's examination room, I stopped being afraid.

A young man dressed like the grandpa was standing at a counter near the window of the room. He had no smile; he stared at me before turning back to the counter.

"Let's take a look," the grandpa said, as he slid a cushioned stool on wheels to the examination table.

Although I was not sure what it was we were looking for, I slid my bum on the edge of the examination table. When I tried to look at what the young man was doing, the grandpa, who was by then sitting on his sliding stool, kept me busy with questions.

"What is your favorite color?" "What flower do you like?" He slipped his hands into stiff beekeeper gloves. "What game do you like to play?"

I answered all the questions until the man with no smile turned around. He held something that looked like it had no purpose. It was as thick as a church candle, as long as a hairbrush. The tip glowed bigger, brighter, more oranger than my Apa's cigarettes. Maybe he is going to curl my hair, I thought.

The grandpa put one hand over my mouth and stretched out

my hand with his other. The man without the smile was very quick. He marked the hand that the grandpa was holding. While the I of myself was fleeing from my body, he pulled my other hand and marked that, too. The I of myself had nowhere else to go but come back to itself. My parents could not save me, and once I thought this thought, I already knew too much.

* * *

The government had been holding lengthy discussions and debates about communist guerrillas, internal security, and identification programs for years. We had heard on the radio about the new Personal Identification Stamp System. The clinical tone of the discussions, with references to certified RNs and state regulated doctors, must have lulled us all into a stupor.

"She's too young," my mother told Raji.

Muni inched towards the living room where I was sitting cross-legged on the floor, half playing with my dolls. My father had bought them in Hong Kong several weeks earlier. The dolls had stiff plastic bodies, peach complexions, and glassy blue eyes that shut when I held them in repose. They were identical except for their hair. Two were blonde; the other three were auburn and black-haired. "What shall I call them?" I had asked Mama. She thought for a bit. "What's your favorite letter?" "A," I said. "Names of continents?" I liked her idea. Asia, Africa, America, Australia, and Europe because Antarctica was too long.

Muni sat on the floor next to me and watched as I fixed Africa's hair. She put her hand out to touch Asia; I yanked the doll away from her. When I saw her reach for Europe, I put my hand over it as a warning and looked her squarely in the eye. She looked over her shoulder to see if the adults were watching. Satisfied that they were busy, she put a hand out like a thief and grabbed America.

"What is one more mouth for a rich woman like you?" Raji asked.

"Crazy laws and big trouble."

"I've watched you for months at the cathedral. You pray very hard. You lay flowers at Francis Xavier's feet," Raji said. "How do you know he didn't send me? Maybe he wants you to repair what they did to my daughter?"

My mother sighed. "I have nothing to do with politics. You think I can change laws?"

"Maybe you can't change big things, but you can take my daughter," Raji said. Her sari made a swishing sound as she retreated towards the door.

Muni dropped America when she heard the accordion gates on the front door squeak open. "Ama!"

"Mem will take care of you." Raji kissed her, once on the forehead, once on the lips, once on each cheek. "Understand?" Raji asked.

"No," Muni whimpered.

"Think how it won't be," Raji said, her hands holding her daughter's shoulders. Muni did not protest as her mother slid the gate shut.

She dragged her cloth bundle by one rabbit's ear as I led her to the guestroom. I held America by one leg, its head pointing to the floor, its knickers showing.

"Are you poor?" I asked.

"I'm dirty only." She looked around the room. "So pretty." She brushed her hands on the lace curtains, running her hands over its embroidered roses.

I sat on the bed. She hopped on beside me. I pulled away when she came too close. I remembered that Mama had asked me to tell Muni about the flushing toilet.

"You don't squat on it like at home, you sit on it like on a chair." I opened the bathroom door. "Like a chair, like a throne, you get it?"

16

Muni walked past me into the bathroom, and sat on the toilet with the seat still up. "Like this?" she asked, before she sank into the bowl. She struggled to rise, stretching her hand out for mine.

"What a fool!" I muttered, as I leaned forward and pulled her up.

She craned her neck to look at her rear end, which was all wet. She walked back to the bedroom holding the wet material of her dress away from her body. "I want to go home," she said quietly.

I offered her my doll.

She sat on the floor and cradled America; it shut its blue eyes. She made it stand, and it opened them. Muni looked up at me, smiling.

I did not like her, but I could not bring myself to ask for America back.

"A Qalit in my house!" My father exploded on the other side of my bedroom wall, as soon as everyone had retired for the night. It was unusual for Papa to talk at all, let alone yell. He was at ease in his silence, sitting in the library, reading his books, composing his speeches, pounding the keys on his typewriter.

I parted the mosquito nets around my bed, arranged Asia and Europe on one side of my pillow, Africa and Australia on the other, and climbed in.

"Have you no morals?" I heard my mother say. Her anger chilled me. She had come into my room earlier, as she did most nights, to release the mosquito nets from their nesting hoop high above my bed and to say my prayers with me. She made a cross on my forehead with her thumb and told me that Muni was our secret, that I must never tell anyone.

"I'm a writing monkey, nothing more," Papa shot back.

"How can you work for people like that, Rohan?"

"It's an identification program," Papa said. "All citizens

carry identification cards. Untouchables are too irresponsible to carry them. PM believes personal stamping is the most efficient system for this group," my father explained, as a press secretary would.

"You're going to burn in hell. Saint Francis will see to it." My mother clicked the light off. I stroked Africa's hair as I listened.

After a few minutes of silence, I heard my father say, "You're my wife. Come on. Come on!"

"No. No. No!"

Within a week, my father did what he had always done after quarreling with my mother: he bowed to her virtue, and the promised wrath of St. Francis. At night, in the weeks and months to come, while I tried to fall asleep, I heard them on the other side of the wall, making love and noises I didn't want to hear.

We settled into a routine at our house. Muni became my mother's little helper. Sita did not object. With America sitting, standing, or lying beside her, Muni made the beds and pushed a long straw broom across the floor. She picked out stones and grit from lentils and rice, and ground spices on a flatbed mortar with a stone rolling pin. When my mother or Sita gave Muni anything more challenging to do, she didn't fare so well. She washed one of my mother's prized handloom gowns in bleach and turned it into a limp, nothing rag. She forgot to separate whites from colors, prompting my father to complain about blue and red underwear for weeks. She left the doors and windows open during a monsoon rain and ruined a rosewood table.

"She's too young," Mama apologized.

"Are we giving her back?" I asked.

"Promises were made," said my mother, at least once a week over the next two years.

Two weeks before the Kennedys arrived, Radio Chomumbhar announced that the Presidential party would be driven from our airport in Sao Domingo through Port Contadu, taking Vasco Da Gama Drive, which hugged Resurrection Beach on the western side of the island, and on to the Prime Minister's retreat at Tilika Peak. The public works department painted all the houses on Da Gama Drive in happy pastel colors especially for the visit. The more hopeless looking *attap* houses were simply barricaded with sky blue corrugated zinc.

We learned that a detail of men incarcerated at Dalimar Prison for hooliganism—a catchall crime that covered everything from extending two-fingered salutes at the Prime Minister to publishing anti-government tracts—would be pressed into service. Lady Lalitha had decided that one day before the visit, the men would hose down all the leaves of trees on the presidential route and spray them with milk to make them look shiny and beautiful.

There were daily bulletins on the radio about which parts of Chomumbhar the Kennedys would see, and which hospitals they would visit. The island's horticultural society named a new strain of orchid—lilac petals with wine-colored dabs—the "Bouvier Blaze." All of Chomumbhar was aroused.

A week before the visit, my father informed us that we would attend a garden party for the Kennedys at Flore de la Mar, the observatory on Tilika Peak. In response, my mother and I went shopping. I remember no intervening moment between my father's announcement and our shopping expedition in Port Contadu. Unable to decide what we would wear, we came home with several choices. A white shantung cheongsam with a dragon of pearls across the bodice, a fitted black sarong with a black bustier draped in purple Balinese lace, and a jeweled red sari for my mother. For me, a pink satin dress with a large bow of shiny purple sateen and matching headband, and a yellow embroidered tunic reaching the thigh, paired with slim pants and a wispy, floral scarf.

We laid the clothes out on the king bed in my parents' room.

Muni stood by the door and watched as we tried on the clothes, and necklaces and chokers from my mother's jewelry box.

"Muni, which one?" I held up two pairs of shoes.

"They are both ugly," she said.

"Help me with the zipper, Muni," Mama said.

Muni ran away. She didn't come downstairs the next morning.

"Maybe she's sick," Mama told Sita.

I was seated at the table in the kitchen eating a breakfast of glutinous rice cakes filled with grated coconut meat and brown sugar.

"Laziness is in her African blood." Sita strained the muscles on her forearm, whisking mix for lentil and rice pancakes.

"She's young, Sita." To me, Mama said, "Go see if she's sick."

I banged several times on Muni's door. "Coming or not?" Not hearing anything, I banged again. "You better come out or you're going to get it."

"Go away. I want to go home. I want my Ama," she yelled.

I ran downstairs to report the incident. My mother looked at Sita, then walked urgently to Muni's room. "Muni, what's wrong with you? Are you sick? Are you bleeding down there?"

"I want my Ama. I want to go home."

My mother and I looked at each other. "I thought you were happy here. We take care of you, don't we?" Mama asked.

"And I share everything with you," I said.

Muni opened the door. She had been crying. She wiped her nose with the back of her sleeve. She looked at me and then at my mother. "Take me to garden party," she said.

My father took his seat in the formal dining room that evening. "Very elaborate," he said, surveying the elaborate spread on the table.

Mama had ordered Sita to cook as if for a wedding.

"A wedding, Madam?" Sita had replied tartly.

"Russians are sending monkeys to the moon. Why is this impossible?" Mama replied. Put that way, Sita outdid herself. Festive yellow rice tinted with turmeric and saffron, medallions of beef simmered in coconut and spices, large prawns on skewers, pomfret baked in banana leaves, five silver boats of vegetables, fraita, pickles, and chutneys, cardamom pudding and layered lapis cake, and a large centerpiece of tiger orchids.

"Celebrating," Mama said, smiling at Papa. She was wearing a red silk blouse and skirt that made her pale skin look flushed and shiny, as if she had a fever. I suspected that the lapel pin skewered her thigh.

Papa and I were in our home clothes of muslin. My father was a delicate man, with a small frame and small bones, but his head was large, his eyes big, and his forehead wide. He has just the right body for a reader and writer, my mother once said to a cousin.

My mother fussed over Papa as she ladled and spooned Sita's wedding-worthy delicacies on his plate. She settled in her seat, and passed me the platters.

"Who could have imagined it? Ummh? The Americans. Here!"

"They are rather special." Papa picked cloves and cinnamon bark from the scented yellow rice and placed them in a bowl. He ate neatly, in small bites, and talked about the latest changes to the Kennedy itinerary. "Lalitha is closing the schools so children can line the route."

"Special for the children too," Mama said, elbow on the table, arm of red silk poised in mid-air, saffron rice on her fork, waiting. "Ummh! I don't know why I didn't think of this before. But Muni should be at the party."

I made my eyes go soft and watery so I could not see. I was not jealous of Muni, but the thin line between holiness and lies that my mother tripped daily because of Muni worried me.

"Outlandish and impossible!" Papa said.

"She could stand in the back, not disturb anybody." She held another forkful to her lips.

"They joke in the Cabinet that they can smell Qalit," he said.

"She won't go within two hundred yards of any of them. She'll be my friend's daughter from Ceylon."

"It won't work," my father said sharply.

"How serious you are," my mother said.

"If we get caught, it won't be a joke will it?" My father used his loud, scolding voice. He looked at me as if appealing to my good sense. His face looked blurry.

"PM loves you. You make him sound important with your big words," Mother said. "He used 'phrontistery' twice last week." Mama offered my father a second helping of cardamom pudding.

"He's an engineer who longs to sound like a philosopher. He doesn't care what it means," Papa said as he scooped it to his lips.

"See? You can do no wrong," Mama said. We ate in silence, except for the noise of spoons scraping against the silver.

"Be careful," my father said, finally.

My mother shrieked with delight. "No purgatory for you. You are going straight to heaven. Saint Francis will see to it." She planted kisses on his head and his hands.

"Tell your saint to keep me out of Dalimar," Papa said.

On the morning of the garden party, Mama and Muni huddled in the tiny bathroom adjoining Muni's room. Muni's hair, freshly washed, hung limp and damp down her back. My mother placed a towel around Muni's shoulders. Muni stood in front of the sink and stared at the mirror, while my mother positioned herself behind her, large scissors in hand.

"Qalit never cut our hair," Muni said.

"Exactly," my mother said, as she held up large bunches of

Muni's hair and cut them above the neck and below the jaw. When she had reduced the bulk, she picked up a smaller pair of trimming shears.

"You must look thoroughly modern," Mama said, as she clipped the thin strands of hair she held between her fingers. She turned Muni around and snipped the hair in front into bangs before drying it.

I was already dressed in the yellow tunic and pants, sitting on Muni's bed, when my mother walked in with several shopping bags.

"Ready, Muni?" Mama placed them on the bed.

Muni, clad only in panties, lingered in the bathroom doorway. She looked like a newborn with her fresh haircut.

Mama fished a white crinoline petticoat from one of the bags. It was tied with ribbons in three places so it looked like a woman's shape. Tossing the ribbons on the bed, Mama bent slightly forward and shook the skirt twice. The skirt flared out like a huge umbrella. Muni stepped into it as if she were afraid of tearing it. Mother handed her my second choice—the pink satin dress with the purple bow. Muni pulled it over her head, twisting her waist this way and that, and pulling the dress down past her hips. While Mama helped her with the zipper, Muni set the pink headband on her head and adjusted its purple crushed velvet rose. She sat on the edge of the bed and pulled on a pair of dainty white socks. She slipped her feet into a pair of my shoes, shiny white with gold buckles.

"What a lady you are," my mother said.

The low dressing table had two tall, swiveling side mirrors and a wider centerpiece. Muni looked in all three mirrors. She saw herself, as well as herself looking at herself.

"Why do you look like that?" I asked.

"I don't want to go," she said.

"It's too late for that now." Mama retrieved a long white box from a drawer. She opened the box and took out a pair of white gloves. It was frilled around the wrists, and piped in the same purple as the bow on Muni's dress.

Much had been done to prepare for our country's turn on the international stage. We had to compensate for the fact that nobody in the world had ever heard of us. The Prime Minister wanted everything to be done in a way that would reflect our dignity as a free people, our character and discipline, and his bold ambition for our country after British rule.

Lady Lalitha had spared no expense in preparing Flore de la Mar for the visit. Even the tall hedges surrounding the mansion were decorated. Small sprigs and bouquets of our most beautiful orchids were pinned to luminescent beige ribbons and tied to the hedges with clear fishing line. The chairs on the lawn, arranged in neat rows in front of a canopied dais, were the color of our blush pearls—eggshell white with pink undertones.

Waiters, wearing black trousers and red jackets with gold epaulets, served flutes of champagne garnished with lychees, and shrimp puffs.

Lady Lalitha greeted my mother. When she looked down her imperious nose at me, I dipped my knee and spread my tunic. We served at her pleasure, Papa had frequently reminded us. It was she who had created the Personal Identification Stamp System, her fifth wedding anniversary gift to herself.

"How grand it all is." Lady Lalitha turned to my mother. She looked resplendent in a pale gold sari studded with gold bugle beads . She dripped in gold and Burmese rubies from her ears, her throat, her fingers, her wrists, and her arms. Her large squished breasts and deep cleavage made me shy.

"Oh, yes, my lady, Chomumbhar will never be the same again," Mama agreed.

"Yes, everything will pale in comparison. And then, whatever will we do?" Lady Lalitha sighed, working her filigreed ivory fan so fast her mammoth breasts heaved with the effort. Her gaze fell on Muni, and she flipped her fan shut with the flick of a wrist.

"A friend's daughter from Ceylon," my mother said quickly.

"Very nicely turned out." Lady Lalitha bopped Muni on the head with her fan.

Eleven stretched to noon, and the Kennedys had still not arrived. We admired the food and the flower arrangements, and strolled indoors to cool ourselves under the overhead fans and to fetch chilled drinks. My mother scolded Muni when she saw her fiddling with the rear of her skirt.

"The petticoat is scratchy," Muni explained.

"Well-bred girls do not stand around picking things out of their bum," my mother said.

The men got louder by the hour as they sipped champagne and wine.

"I pray they get here soon, while we're still respectable," the Health Minister's wife told Mama.

"Yes, pray," said my mother, eyeing the Health Minister, who appeared to be medicating himself with whiskey.

Lady Lalitha walked quickly to my mother. "The little one, I must have her."

"My daughter is outside," Mama said.

"No, the other one."

One of the PM's assistants found Muni and brought her to the First Lady.

"You will come with me," Lady Lalitha commanded. "Did anyone ever teach you how to curtsy?" she asked, guiding Muni past the French doors and into the garden.

"Oh, God," my mother said, looking about the room for my father.

A little after one o'clock, a Navy Guard in ceremonial uniform appeared at the French doors, and chimed a triangle. "The car bearing the President and First Lady of the United

States of America is winding up Tilika Peak. Please form a reception line outside according to rank and station."

It was easy, of course. We all knew where we stood in the scheme of things. The PM and Lady Lalitha would be first, then my father, because he gave the Prime Minister's words wings, and by extension us, followed by the deputy Prime Minister, the full Cabinet, and finally, the assorted hierarchy of bureaucrats.

How young and how lucky they looked. Mrs. Kennedy wore jade green raw silk: a scooped neck tunic and a *kebaya* with slits from knee to ankle. Swanlike, she was.

As for the President, the Chomumbhar sun had sealed him in a translucent bronze.

It was afternoon and the sun was overhead, yet they looked dewy and fresh, as if they were taking an autumn stroll in New England instead of sweating it out a few yards from the Equator. They were too everything—exotic, blessed, much.

My father, my mother, and I took our assigned chairs on the lawn on the first row. The two "First" couples sat on the proscenium in maharajah chairs with opulent backs.

We listened to the Prime Minister's speech—my father's speech—welcoming the President and his wife. He compared the three thousand-year history of Chomumbhar to the two hundred-year story of America. "We are both a nation of immigrants … America's youth and vitality propel it to the sun and the moon, while our ancient story pulls us back to the sea and the earth … There are perfections and flaws in both our philosophies … We need to imagine new possibilities for our nations," Prime Minister D'Souza read from the prepared text. Once he had finished, he looked uncertain. He looked at my father as if to ask, "What the hell do I mean, flaws? New possibilities?"

My father stood up and clapped energetically. Lady Lalitha and my mother followed suit. Everyone else soon joined in. The PM nodded awkwardly, then bowed to the President and First Lady. Still seated, they clapped politely.

My mother squeezed my father's hand.

When the clapping died down, Lady Lalitha stepped up to the microphone and welcomed the visitors to Chomumbhar, "the island of pearls and dreams." She signaled Muni.

Muni walked stiffly towards the dais. Lady Lalitha handed Muni a large bouquet of Bouvier Blaze. Muni, filled with the solemnity of the occasion, turned like a soldier and presented Mrs. Kennedy with the bouquet. At Lady Lalitha's nod, Muni curtsied.

Mrs. Kennedy asked Muni how old she was and what grade she was in.

Muni blinked and replied, "Thank you."

Flash bulbs popped.

"And what do you plan to be when you grow up?" The President leaned forward, and took Muni's gloved hand.

"Someone else, Mr. President," said Muni.

His eyes creased with laughter as he turned to his wife. She drew a hand to her lips to stifle a giggle.

Things changed in a day.

The Empty Hour

The newest seamstress at Li Li Loong's Fashion House rotated her aching shoulders. She lifted the clamp on her electric sewing machine to release a finished garment. "No more." She stood up roughly, her aluminum chair scraping across the red tile floor.

"Ugh!" Mah Mei, the storyteller, interrupted her story about the beautiful but unlucky Princess Hong Li Po. "You're spoiling everyone's pleasure."

Mah Mei was seated in front of a semi-circle of dressmakers and their humming machines. Her rattan chair was planted on a rug quilted from Li Li's scrap fabrics. Two wooden crates stood erect by Mah Mei's side, one on top of the other. They held Wu Lai epics, Qin philosophies, tea tales, folk sagas, romances, and autobiographies.

"Your stories are horrible." The girl pulled a band off her ponytail and shook her head like a woman in a shampoo commercial.

"What did you say?" Mah Mei narrowed her eyes and puckered her lips. She was a bird of a woman, small and thin, as if she had folded herself in half. Her sixty-year-old face was marked with deep furrows from a lifetime of brooding at the tragedy of her own life.

"Your voice is like a squealing pig in labor." The girl inserted a hanger through the sleeves of the finished dress.

"Insolent girl!" Mah Mei turned to Li Li. "Do you hear how she abuses me?"

Li Li Loong was at her post behind a counter that ran from

one edge of the shop wall to the other. She was a sturdy, thick-bodied woman of forty-five, with round features and short black hair cut like a man's. Her face was grave, as always. She sat on a high chair like a barstool, the better for supervising her seamstresses. She glanced at Mah Mei and the girl before looking down at her red ledger.

"Old age used to count for something," Mah Mei said. "In my day, we were humble. Now they don't even know what Tao is or what the precepts are."

"Keeping your mouth shut is a good precept," the girl said.

The other seamstresses laughed in agreement, except for Ng, who was hunched over a large table in the center of the room sewing glass beads to a finished gown. Though nearly thirty, she looked like a young girl, waif-like and without curves. She had a striking crop of glossy black hair that settled around her shoulders like a cloak and covered her eyes.

Mah Mei shut the book in dramatic fashion. "Lao Tsu says, 'Know you are innocent, remain steadfast when insulted, and be a valley for all under heaven,'" she said, walking towards the kitchen, chin held high, her face composed like a martyr.

Li Li looked at Mah Mei's retreating back, stared at the girl, and went back to checking figures in her ledger. Their concerns were not her concern. As long as their fighting didn't interfere with her business of making money, she didn't see the harm. She counted the day's cash receipts. Her right hand flew over the beads of a large black abacus. Ssshhh. The beads clicked against each other as they added up her fortune. Ssshhh. She folded two large bills, tucked them into her bra, and glanced around the room.

"Stop hiding yourself. What's wrong with you?" she yelled at Ng in Hakka, a dialect understood by no one else in the room but Ng.

Ng continued sewing without looking at Li Li.

Li Li lifted the flap of the counter and marched towards Ng.

29

When Ng straightened herself up from the table, Li Li looked at her sharply.

"Show yourself." Li Li pushed Ng's hair roughly off her face. "Suffer when you're alone," she scolded the girl. It made Li Li angry to see Ng lose herself inside the dresses, sending herself too far away and deep inside her own head.

"Who wishes for me to describe Hong Li Po's marriage to King Manzur of Malaya?" Mah Mei asked, returning from the kitchen to her seat.

"What's to describe about marriage?" one seamstress asked wearily.

"To which, furthermore, she was sold by her father," said her friend.

As Mah Mei read the tale of Princess Hong Li Po, aluminum chairs in numbers began to scrape against the red floor. One by one, all of Li Li's workers stood up from their sewing stations. The women tilted their necks from side to side, arched their backs, or massaged their necks and shoulders to undo an afternoon's hard labor. They did not put their work away, organize their sewing caddies, or sweep the fabric remnants lying on the floor like afterbirth, the way they did each night before Li Li closed the shop.

Mah Mei stopped reading.

"Don't stop. Tell us about her handmaidens," cried one of the Foo sisters, the one who drew black liner in the space where brow bone ended and eye socket began, to create eyelids.

"Idiot! Empty Hour already," the Foo mother scolded her daughter.

The Empty Hour was that space in the afternoon between two and three when people in Chomumbhar retired from industry. If they were at offices, they'd break for frothy iced coffee laced with condensed milk, or chilled mung bean soup, or banana fritters; or they'd peel open the Island Mail, the local newspaper that reported everything on how to behave and nothing about what was going on. If people were at home, they would lie down to beat the heat. Children already home from school would take off their stiff government-issue uniforms and put on their home clothes: shirts and dresses of the thinnest voile that traced the lines of the body, and soft cotton shorts and pants of muslin, so light they hung like air against skin. They would curl up in bed with a toy, a book, their mothers, or their *ayahs*, and drift off to sleep.

Li Li's workers, even the ones with grumpy faces, always brightened at the nearness of the Empty Hour. They seemed to look forward to it, not as a rest break so much as a cure for their ailments. They talked about their Empty Hour plans that consisted variously of going upstairs to their living quarters to sleep, shower, groom themselves, or change into fresh clothes. When they returned to the shop at three, the cheap smells of 4711 Eau de Cologne, "for refreshing the spirit," according to the label, and Hazeline Snow, "for cooling the tropical complexion," and Cuticurra Talc, "for keeping the particulars and extremities dry," wafted in after them and lingered in the air like storm clouds. It did not escape Li Li's notice that after the Empty Hour they seemed less angry with their lot in life, and appeared to forget, momentarily anyway, the very real fact that Li Li exploited them daily.

"I will read you *tanka* about empty hours." Mah Mei held up a slim volume, a final effort to keep her audience. "I stand as though only I am existing in heaven and earth, at this solitariness you are smiling, coming stealthily. Who is it hitting the temple bell? It is late and time for even the Buddha to go into dreaming. In the Lord Buddha's drowsy eyes, the ancient country fields have their hazy existence."

"*Lau yah*—so horrible!" said the Foo sister with the pencil tricks.

"*Chee bhai!*" said the mother.

The other Foo sister cackled at her mother's exclamation for vagina.

Several of Li Li's workers disappeared into the kitchen at the back of the shop.

Li Li always marveled at the sweets they would concoct for the Empty Hour. A few days before, they had produced bowls of volcano—shaved ice mountains, their hollows filled with red beans, black jelly, and condensed milk. Another time, they unwrapped an agar-agar jelly dyed to resemble a watermelon: green for the outer shell, frothy egg white for the membrane, pink food coloring for the fruit, and pumpkin seeds for the seeds.

The rest of the women filed upstairs to their living quarters. Living quarters was a lie, too grand-sounding for what Li Li actually gave them. What she provided were chicken coops for her egg-laying seamstresses. They occupied the four floors between Li Li's shop in the basement and her apartment on the fifth floor. In the coops, there were mattresses on the floor, fifty mattresses in all, arranged in configurations of fours, fives, and sixes in each room. The newest tenants in the chicken coops slept on the 'highway,' the long corridor cutting through the middle of each floor from front door to back door. Highway occupants were treated like cats. If they were sleeping, others on their way to the bathrooms at each end of the house swept the sleeping bodies aside with their feet, or stepped over them without asking them to move. Although the entire shop house belonged to Li Li, she never went upstairs to the chicken coops. Her business was confined to the shop and the fifth floor, where she lived.

To hear the local gossip, Li Li Loong hadn't been the same since someone had commissioned a charm on her. Nobody knew the details of how Li Li was charmed, but various methods were discussed. Some people said Moy, her former boss, had grown so jealous of her success that he had buried a charm in front of the shop. The charm, it was said, consisted of an old black-and-white photograph of Li Li, bunches of her hair, and the eye of a dead bull. The dull eye was to represent unseeing, to give Li Li a blindness that had no cure. Li Li herself had given credence to this method by telling people that someone had broken into her flat and stolen her photographs. Others speculated that the charm was buried in the shop, suggesting a vendetta by one of her workers or collaboration with Moy. They talked about how Li Li's yellow complexion was no longer yellow, but a light brown. She is possessed by a Malay demon, was the general conclusion. They also considered how she walked differently, not like a woman at all, the way she used to, in small, quick steps, but large, mannish steps with hands swinging in big arcs like a lorry driver. "The demon possessing her is a man," people whispered.

To be sure, the old Li Li was a successful person fully in control of everything. Everyone on the island knew of Li Li's ability to turn nothing into something, how she was able to exploit every situation and make a profit.

Li Li was a duck. She had started out like all the other ducks—Chinese illegals who had paid the Snakeheads to navigate them across the Pacific Ocean, the South China Sea, the Indian Ocean, the Straits of Malacca. Depending on what the ducks could afford, the Snakeheads secreted them in wooden shipping containers on cargo freighters, small fishing boats, or even rowboats, and smuggled them out of China. The ducks often washed up on Chomumbhar. Usually, they were heading to Malaysia, Singapore, Australia, or New Zealand, but landed on the island after being pushed off course by the winds.

Li Li had paid the Snakeheads five thousand *yuan*, with an additional five thousand to be paid once she was successfully landed on the island. For fifteen thousand more and a promissory note for twenty thousand, the Snakeheads had told her they would smuggle her into America, into Chinatown in New York or San Francisco. But she hadn't had that kind of money.

Li Li waited eleven weeks before the Snakeheads came to her house and told her to be ready that night. They were very specific: bring two large bottles, a thin necked one like a soy sauce bottle, filled with drinking water, and a big, wide one like a pickle jar for making toilet. They instructed her to fill a soft cloth bag, that would not make rustling noises, with dried plums, dried ginger, and sesame cookies. Don't bring anything else, they told her.

She was hidden in a crate surrounded by bags of rice. It was wide enough for Li Li to stretch her hands from end to end, but only tall enough to crouch in. It had finger widths of space between the cheap wood covered in splinters. Loaded onto a lorry driven by a Snakehead, the crate was part of a container shipment of rice from her province, headed for Indonesia and Chomumbhar.

As smuggling journeys go, Li Li's was an uneventful one. Her crate was placed in a shady part of the ship, surrounded by other crates packed tight with rice, and without a footpath anywhere near it. She was a stowaway with millions of grains of rice, and nobody knew the difference. She could hear the ship hands on deck at all hours of the day and night, yet nobody came near her crate. But she had to be careful all the same. Any sound that was of a different or higher frequency, that stood out above all the other sounds on a ship, would have been suspect. Li Li learned to control everything—the sound of her breathing, her sleeping, her sneezing, her hunger pangs, her elimination. She made sure to go to the toilet only during the day, when there were all kinds of sounds to cover up her own. She never went at night, when the ship was on autopilot and the deck hands stood at the rails, smoking cigarettes, staring at the black water and communing with the moon.

When Li Li landed on the island several weeks later,

Snakeheads unloaded the containers onto a wholesaler's truck. They took her to a Cantonese businessman named Moy, who hired her as a seamstress for his clothing factory. But from the beginning, most of her earnings went to the Snakeheads to pay off her debt. "What's the use?" she would ask herself as the Snakeheads came each week to collect her wages from Moy. She often thought of ways to break away from Moy. Sometimes she thought she would simply kill herself.

The opportunity to free herself arrived five monsoons later, when she learned that the President and First Lady of the United States would be visiting Chomumbhar, a stopover on their way to India. She hatched a plan to steal six yards of fabric from Moy. The jade green silk she had in mind was one of a kind, so special it was wrapped in tissues, sealed in a plastic bag, and locked inside a glass cabinet in Moy's storeroom.

During that Empty Hour, Li Li, under pretext of replenishing her stock of threads and notions, forced the lock open with a thick craft needle. She wrapped the cloth tightly around her body under the folds of her loose smock, and worked that way until the end of her shift.

That week, Moy gave his seamstresses two days off so that they could have a four-day weekend for the Moon Festival. Li Li locked the door of the bathroom in Moy's chicken coop, and sat in the bathtub. Measuring tape snaked around her neck, scissors propped on her knees, and pins pressed between her lips, Li Li went to work on the cloth. "Escape or die," she promised herself, as she proceeded to sew all her hopes into that piece of jade green cloth.

"Li Li, I need to do my business," "Li Li, I need to piss bad," her fellow seamstresses whined from the other side of the door.

"Use bottle!" Li Li shouted back, as she cut and folded, nipped and tucked, and stitched all the pieces of the jade green silk. Front left bodice to back left panel, front right bodice to back right panel, front left peplum to back peplum to front right peplum. Right sleeve to tunic, left sleeve to tunic. Skirt front panel to skirt back panel.

Li Li sewed the entire garment by hand, using a tiny needle so small it barely had an eye, and fine silk threads that matched the cloth. When the gown was finished, Li Li stitched the words "Li Li Loong, Best Dressmaker" on the inside of the garment in gold thread.

She wrapped the *kebaya* in crackling white tissue, placed it in a good box that Moy reserved for his better customers, and addressed it to First Lady Mrs. Kennedy.

"First Lady want to wear native dress when she come," Li Li lied with a stone face to the stone-faced Marine at the gate of the U.S. Consulate on Embassy Row.

The Ambassador's wife handed the First Lady the box on the day the Kennedys went to the Ambassador's house for tea. Mrs. Kennedy took a liking to the thing and wore it to an official function, a garden party at the observatory on Tilika Peak. The photograph of Mrs. Kennedy wearing Li Li Loong's kebaya is part of everyone's family album on the island. It also appeared in Time and Life magazines, and newspapers around the world, next to the one of her in India, taken three days later, wearing a mini skirt and sitting on an elephant. Li Li became famous as the First Lady's dressmaker, and every woman on the island wanted to be dressed by Li Li Loong.

The seamstresses at Loong's wore yellow poplin tunics and pants that Li Li had designed herself. Nothing could be hidden in the loosely woven, stiff cloth that neither draped nor folded, reducing the likelihood of Li Li's workers stealing her expensive inventory of fabrics and notions. Hand-woven shantung, yardages of silks so fine they folded inside the closed palm of a hand, wool harvested from the beards of native hill sheep, and embellishments of glass beads, tiger's eye, azure, and freshwater pearls. Li Li's life depended on them.

Young, middle-aged, old, the Chinese women were different from each other, and essentially themselves only from the face up. They were an odd bunch. The plain ones gravitated to each other to form a larger assembly of plain. The pretty ones walked with their hands around each other's waists, behaving as one would in the newness of love. And the old women forged into their own group, sharing only their silence and exhaustion. Their vitality, the *chi* of them, declined with the number of years they had worked in Li Li's shop. The newest seamstress was full of spit and fire, but it was only a matter of time before her *chi* would be sapped, and she too learned to know and take her place. The younger ones became inseparable from others in their clique, often forgetting they were single, independent, freestanding individuals. If Li Li asked one of them to fetch spools of thread from the storage room, or cut cloth laid under tissue paper patterns, the whole group would respond as if they were one person. Only Mah Mei and Ng, who did not speak, lacked affiliation to any of the groups.

There were fifty workstations in all, five across, and ten running down the length of the shop, spreading like a fan across the room. All the machines were occupied except the third machine in row three; it had been Mah Mei's. But Li Li had relieved Mah Mei of her duties, after her hands quit on her from arthritis, and she could barely turn the feeder on her machine, or sew a straight seam without groaning. By that time, business was so good that Li Li did not complain about Mah Mei's disability. Even so, Mah Mei always made a point of looking busy enough to earn her keep. She would arrive at the shop before the others and spend the rest of the day making a big show of dusting, sweeping, organizing the bales and rolls of fabrics and notions, and fetching inventory from the storeroom. She also began to fetch tea and water for everyone in the shop.

The other seamstresses complained to Li Li about Mah Mei. "Hai yah! She pokes her big, fat nose in our work. We cannot find anything. Everything takes twice as long."

To each other, they complained about how they were chained to their machines, now that they could no longer loiter in the storeroom or kitchen.

"You will be storyteller," Li Li announced one morning, as Mah Mei stood at Li Li's counter separating five kinds of buttons into transparent bins. "It will be up to you to soothe them, make them happy and peaceful, make their days go faster."

Mah Mei took her new role seriously. The first story she read to the seamstresses was *The Tale of Genji*. For days she read the Japanese novel and failed to get a response from the women. Not a smile, or a look of encouragement, or an acknowledging nod. They closed their ears to her story, and continued to sew and cut and examine their work with poker faces, as if she had assaulted them. They were sour like curdled milk, but she was determined to win them over. She took great care to modulate her voice when she read. She took deep breaths and held her stomach and rectum tight, and smiled with her eyes, so that her Cantonese would sound pleasant and full of light and music. She measured her words and released them carefully, like thread from a spool, now fast, now a little slower, now in a hush.

"This is the world's first novel," she told them each morning as she picked up the book. "A woman wrote it. She knew all about the human heart."

When the seamstresses continued to occupy themselves with their work, not even looking at Mah Mei when she thought her reading especially fine, she felt her own spirits crumble. She heard her own voice that she had once imagined dripping in green honey tea, so sweet and musical she believed it to be, turn into a pathetic drone, shrill and tuneless. On the fifth day of entering the world of Lady Murasaki, she came upon a string of words, a shimmering lapidary. "'Again and again, something in one's own life, or in the life around one, will seem so important that one cannot bear to let it pass into oblivion. There must never come a time, the writer feels, when people do not know about this.'" She read the words to them once, twice, and then again, and each time the words made her feel sadly happy, happily sad.

You always started out with worry when you went to Loong's for a dress. You didn't know anything: not what you wanted, not how it looked, not how it was going to make you feel, and not if it was going to be worth all the trouble.

"What for you want?" was the first and most important question Li Li asked her customers. Answering it truthfully made all the difference. If you didn't, you would end up with a dress made without care or feeling. If you opened up and confessed why you really wanted the dress—because you wanted your lover to leave his wife, or because you wanted to forget that you were poor, or because you wanted your husband of too many years to kiss you on the lips and part your legs in hunger and taste you as if you were new to him—Loong's workers would make you a talisman dress. This wondrous thing would do for you all that you wanted it to.

"What new designs are you dreaming up?" you might ask Li Li.

"Depends," she would say as her fingers flew over an abacus with huge black wooden beads.

"On what?"

"On what for," she'd mumble as she tallied her fortune in a thick, dog-eared ledger.

If you made yourself humble, there was hope. "To fix my bad luck," you might say.

Li Li's eyes would stare as she set her abacus aside. "I have grand design I see only with third eye," she'd say, tapping the middle of her forehead.

Li Li spoke an English that was direct and without decoration. "Make you look like fat buffalo arse," Li Li would tell large women intent on horizontal stripes. "For sure this design make mosquito bites look like breasts," or "Man come back when he see you in this dress," she would say, praising customers who agreed to her choice of fabric and design.

One of the senior dressmakers would take charge of you. You hoped it would be either Lim or Cheong, and not Ng.

"Why doesn't she talk?" a customer who was unaware of Ng's condition might ask.

"She only speak Hakka," Li Li would say. Li Li had decided to learn Hakka when the Snakeheads began bringing girls from the Southern provinces.

"No more words inside her. Her baby died." Mah Mei would contradict Li Li.

"Don't tell ugly story," Li Li would scold Mah Mei.

Nevertheless, if customers pressed Mah Mei, she would tell the story despite Li Li's loud objections.

"I don't want to hear that story," Li Li would yell at Mah Mei.

"It will be good for you to hear it," Mah Mei would say. Then she would tell Ng's story. "Wrapped at her chest in two cloths twisted and tied together at her hips, she carried her new baby. Good baby, never cried, even with the rocking of the boat and the sun so hot. Near Labu, the boat with two men, one woman, and her baby, ran out of food and then water. 'It's only a girl. Let her be good for something,' the men scolded her. Three days without food, and nothing to drink. The sound of baby feasting on milk made them very angry. On fourth day, she woke up to tugs on her baby wraps, the men pulling this way and that. 'It's only a girl.' They threw the baby into the water. They lived on mother's milk until they reached the island."

As for Ng, she did not speak.

Li Li despised the Empty Hour. To her, it was the hour

of reckoning and regretting, the hour of sweat and fatalism. Nevertheless, since all on the island practiced this foolishness of extended loafing, Li Li had no choice but to fold up her business as well. She took the day's takings, three hundred *flores* in large bills, and ran her long money-counting thumbnail and forefinger along their fold. When the *flores* were sufficiently pressed, she slipped them into the cups of her bra. She locked the street entrance to the shop and walked down the narrow dirt and grass path on the side of it. When she turned the corner and reached the back of the building, she stroked the wad of money attached to her bosom. She climbed the unsteady fire escape, gripping the rails tightly until she reached the landing on the fifth floor. She closed the door behind her before bending over to settle her racing heart.

"Loong too old for this shit," she mumbled as she slumped into a blue vinyl sofa. All the furniture in Li Li's living room was lumped senselessly close together in the middle of it, while a wide path of wasted space made a border around the room.

"So easy for you," Li Li said, staring at a statue of the Buddha on the coffee table. It was a cheap reproduction of the giant Reclining Buddha of Shwethalyaung in Burma, which was reputed to be fashioned entirely of gold, gold leaf, and precious gems.

Li Li had found hers in a rubbish heap in the back of her shop. Most likely, one of her seamstresses had lost something big and blamed her god for being too small. And most likely, when this small god didn't help her find her big lost thing, she threw him out. Although Li Li didn't believe in any god, she admired it. The Buddha was a foot long, carved out of a single piece of wood and painted in gold. Its robes, also fashioned from the wood, flowed gracefully like real cloth. The robe's hem and borders were encrusted with fake stones that looked like diamonds, rubies, sapphires, and emeralds. Its eyes were unseeing, lost in contemplation.

Li Li liked the way the Gautama lay—on his side, his head

resting in the cupped palm of one hand, his other hand resting lightly about the thigh. Li Li didn't know how to lie around; that was her big problem. She remembered the tape measure draped around her neck and flung it on the table in front of her. For no apparent reason, she picked up the tape measure and measured both her wrists. "You're crazy," she scolded herself. She leaned back against the lumps on her sofa, stared at the Buddha, and took a long breath. It is late and time for even the Buddha to go into dreaming. Li Li liked the thought.

"Today, Loong will bow to the Empty Hour," she said aloud.

Li Li pushed aside the beaded curtain on her bedroom door and kicked her clogs off. Clog and clog—the wooden shoes slid into each other across the linoleum. The room was small, neat. A dark, wooden folding screen with three panels divided the room from the bathroom. Hanging over the screen was a bath towel and a floral-patterned robe, its flowers dead from too many washes. A twin bed without a headboard was pushed lengthwise against the exterior wall. A large window, the Asian kind, with two wood frames, opened out onto the roof from the wall between bed and bathroom. Next to the window stood a dresser with a low table and stool. Li Li opened the window frames and parted the curtains.

She walked back towards the beaded curtain and turned a dial on the wall. She watched the ceiling fan churn slowly to life. Li Li carefully turned the knob to a spot marked "med oss," her ideal setting, although she did not know it meant medium oscillation.

"Loong will go to sleep." She lay down on the bed. But she didn't mean it.

Li Li curled up, then stretched out, and then changed the direction of her sleep. She lay face down with her head hanging off the bed, then with her feet up, parallel to the wall. But her thoughts raced, no matter how she tried to still them. She lay flat on her back and followed the spokes of the ceiling fan with her eyes. "Loong very tired. Loong very sleepy," she said, trying to hypnotize herself. But each time, a thought would rise from her head like smoke from a mosquito coil, hover over her, and finally float to the ceiling fan. It was useless, she had no peace. Half past the Empty Hour, Li Li sat at the dressing table and looked in the mirror. It gave her back a disappointment, a woman used up like a finished glass of ice water. Her head was full of thoughts. She could not stop thinking about herself and her lack of things, the ones that had no price and could not be bought with money fished from her bra. Li Li had been through a lot, but the simple things had escaped her. She had never been with anyone, man or woman, to a coffee bar, or the stalls at Change Alley, or for a walk on Resurrection Beach. She had never talked on the telephone with anyone about things other than business. She had never known a man. No one other than her mother had ever said *wo ai ni* to her. She seemed always to have been at the wrong place when she needed something basic. Even back in China, when she should have been sharing time with friends or entertaining suitors, there was no one there. All the young people were on their way to somewhere else. People thought that she was retarded because she was sixteen and still in the place where was born. She turned away from the mirror in disgust.

Only fifteen minutes until the end of the Empty Hour: the alarm clock on Li Li's dressing table promised relief. As Li Li wondered what to do with herself till then, she saw something flutter past the window. She was sure it was a shadow or a ghost, because she had felt a big fear land on her heart when it passed, like a lizard falling from the ceiling. She thought immediately of the charm: the Malay male demon was stalking her.

She stuck her head out the window. There was nothing to see on the roof, just television antennas, telephone poles, and her clothes and sheets drying on several lines strung to wooden stakes in the cement floor. The mouth of an alley began in front of Li Li's building, cut through two rows of shophouses, and ended near a canvas of blue in the distance. Li Li was about to close the window when she heard noises, the demon walking around.

"I will call the demon slayer," Li Li hollered.

The sheets on the line flew up in the breeze, like a woman's skirt billowing up around her waist to show her panties. Li Li saw Ng standing in front of the wall, looking out at the Indian Ocean.

"Are you stupid?" Li Li shouted. "Only crazy people outside at this hour."

Before Li Li could say another word, it started to rain, heavy and all at once. Ng didn't move. "Crazy girl, come inside." Li Li put her hand out to Ng, who was soaking like a rag by then.

Ng walked slowly to the window, took Li Li's hand and climbed in.

"Look at you, shivering like a beggar." Li Li stared at Ng, angry for no reason other than to be angry. Ng stood motionless, dripping all over Li Li's floor.

"What is wrong with you?" Li Li asked, grabbing the towel hanging over the screen. She ran it roughly over the girl's wet face, her hair, and her body. "Put this on." She handed Ng the flowery robe, and pushed her towards the bathroom door.

Li Li lay on the bed, one hand over her forehead. It was raining steadily now, but the sun was shining. Li Li had to shield her eyes from the prismatic bands of sun pouring in through the window.

"Sun and rain?" Ng asked, as she stood at the foot of Li Li's bed squinting at the stream of light.

Li Li smiled at the voice—pretty, like clean, clear running water. "Monkey's marriage," she said, picking up the nonsensical rhyme children on the island knew by heart.

"Sun and rain, wasteful but welcome," Ng said.

"I don't know the rest." Li Li stood up.

"Something to do with laughing and crying," Ng said.

"You hold your bad luck inside you for too long."

"Empty Hour no good for me," Ng replied. Her still-damp hair, separated into tips, looked like the stems of the faded flowers on the robe.

"No good for anybody with big thoughts." Li Li walked towards Ng.

Ng stepped back.

Li Li took Ng's hand. She guided Ng to the bed and stretched her out on it.

She stroked Ng's hair the way her mother had stroked hers, back in Fujian, when she was a little girl. Li Li lay down next to Ng in silence.

They stared at the fan, at its medium oscillation.

"Am I good dressmaker?" Ng asked.

"Not as good as me, but still good," said Li Li.

"I wish I knew how to stitch myself up," Ng said.

Li Li sat up and stared at Ng. Sometimes hole so big only way is to jump in, she could have told her. Instead, she took the money out of her bra and placed it on the side table. She lay down on the bed like her reclining Buddha, and pressed her thumb on Ng's third eye. And they both bowed to the Empty Hour.

The Ambassador's Wife

Eve Mallon was trying to think of one reason why she couldn't walk away from the breakfast table, and from her husband, Andrew. He had told her, after the second pot of coffee had arrived from the kitchen, that their upcoming ski vacation in Gulmarg, India, would have to be postponed, as the State Department had recently telexed an advisory against Americans traveling to Kashmir. Andrew Mallon knew these things because he was America's Ambassador to Chomumbhar.

The morning had begun as mornings always did at the embassy compound on Tilika Heights—under a large umbrella mushrooming from a wrought-iron table in the back patio of the Mallons' bungalow. Eve drifted in and out of a reverie: speeding down the slopes, wind in her hair, biting cold stinging her cheeks, white powder dusting her lashes and lips.

Andrew was reading the *New York Times,* punctiliously shipped in from the embassy in Sydney, but five to seven days old all the same. The awareness that life had already happened and little of it mattered anymore lent Andrew an air of detachment and serenity, making him look younger than his forty years. The headline that three hundred peasants were massacred in Indochina on the fifth, six days ago, moved him not at all—it was history. The previous week, he had let slip his philosophy of forgetfulness, when his tennis partner, Amer Ayub, consul general of Pakistan, mentioned a particularly gruesome recent bombing in a square in Saigon.

"Did you read the dispatch by Thomas Fowler in *The London Times?*" the consul general asked.

"Oh, I'm not involved," Andrew replied.

"What do you mean, you're not involved?"

"It's all over before it gets to me. Since it's all history anyway, there's nothing I can do about it," Andrew said.

"How wonderful it must be to walk between rain drops," Amer Ayub had said, which would have stung anyone other than Andrew Mallon.

Aini, the Malay servant, set scrambled eggs, bread with *kaya* and a fruit compote on the table. She ignored Eve, smiled at the Ambassador, said *lagi*—later, and left on her morning trek for provisions to Change Alley. The fault was Eve's alone. The offspring of Polish-American immigrants who had been one breath away from destitution, she was mortified by the whole idea of servants and wouldn't look Aini or any of the other help in the eye. She never ate any of the food Aini placed in front of her each morning at breakfast: filigreed pewter dishes with quiches, soufflés, and rotis served with colorful local fruit salads of mangosteen, papaya, and rambutan, garnished with edible flowers. While Andrew polished off everything on his plate and complimented the kitchen staff for their efforts, Eve drank black coffee and smoked cigarettes in silence. When the dishes were returned to the kitchen, Aini and the other maids would shake their heads contemptuously as they examined Eve's plate. Usually, there would be four or five lipstick-ringed cigarette stubs nestled under the fruit or pushed into the eggs. Aini and her staff had worked for several diplomats from Europe and Asia, and they all agreed that Eve Mallon should never have left her own country.

The island was lovely in its own way, but Eve couldn't take the heat. After eighteen years of following her husband from one hot and dusty country to another, she wanted a cold climate. She longed for the Minnesota winters of her childhood. And though she had never been to Poland, she imagined that she would have been in her element there, just as well as in Minneapolis. On the island, "a few feet from the Equator," people hardier than her often joked, Eve's pale skin cringed from the sun and her teary blue eyes grew ever more teary, making her feel she was submerged in water. She was forced to wear sunglasses nearly all the time, which did not endear her to the islanders either: "What is she hiding?"

By mid-morning, Eve would retreat to an Adirondack chair under the arches of the verandah on the side of the house. Beyond the three arches she could see the flowerbeds. There were six long rows with shrubs of ornamental cabbages and pink -centered heart leaves (in every way a heart except for the green edges); white frangipani and orange hibiscus behind them; and flanking the rear, purple and spider orchids and bougainvillea in three notes of red, trained around wooden stakes driven into the ground.

Eve stared at the front and back pages of Andrew's paper as she sipped coffee. "And what's on your agenda this morning?" Andrew lowered his paper onto the table. There was sarcasm in his voice. "Will you be joining the British delegation at the Red Cross tea? Visiting an orphanage? Representing us at the badminton finals, perhaps?" He found that shaming her was often an effective release for his anger.

"There's the packing to be done, isn't there?" she asked. Her chin quivered. Lately, she had also noticed a twitch below her eye, the beating wings of a moth on her cheek. It was as if every sad feeling in her body was manifesting itself on the surface of her skin. She wondered if it was Andrew who made her sick.

"Yes. About that—" he said, as if he had just remembered. He folded the paper four times into a neat package, and then he told her about the travel ban to Kashmir.

"It isn't fair," she said, biting her lip.

"For god's sake, Eve." Andrew stood and pulled the waist of his trousers up.

It was one of the things he did in their marriage: dismiss her feelings by making her seem unreasonable and hysterical.

"Pull yourself together. Get over it." He picked up his paper and turned around to leave.

"It's always something, isn't it?" she asked his retreating back. "Everything I want is somehow the wrong thing." It wasn't just about Kashmir; she had thought that marrying Andrew would guarantee her protection from cruelty. To realize it wasn't true grieved her.

He turned and looked at her sharply. He slapped the paper on his thigh, hard enough to elicit a *thwack* sound. "Yes, but you are selfish and greedy."

"Stop! The servants will hear," she said. "I have to supervise these people."

Andrew laughed. "Supervise! When have you ever supervised anything?"

It wasn't right that he should treat her so badly, but she found her voice. "Don't laugh at me!"

"Everyone laughs at you. It is all over the island that you are quite mad, a sorry example of America," he said.

It baffled Andrew that she didn't know anything at all about being American in the world. He knew that there was no room for individual wants; his job, and hers, was to be American and represent and advance American interests where they stood. That she failed to understand that after all these years amazed him.

Seeing the anger on her husband's face just then, Eve doubted herself. Perhaps he was right after all. There was something terribly wrong with her, a languor, a listlessness that prevented her from going to teas, cutting ribbons, posing next to winning horses at the race track, or smiling for the society pages of the local newspaper.

"It's the heat. I'm not made for this weather. I thought we'd be in London or Rome by now." She stretched out a hand to him: meet me halfway, it pleaded. It was a measure of Eve's lack of a center that she caved in to Andrew so often. But she couldn't help it; she was completely without guile.

"You're a disgrace," he said, before disappearing inside the house. It was true that he was a mediocre diplomat with no facility for making connections, no talent for advocating for himself, no guts to approach the king makers at the State Department for favors, and no flair for accomplishment. It nagged at him daily that he had been assigned to the bottom of the world instead of London or Rome. But he didn't need to hear it, especially from his irresponsible, selfish, unstable wife.

Eve pushed her sunglasses above her head and wiped her eyes with the pads of her fingers. When she adjusted her glasses back on her face, she felt her body slump into a surrender.

Eve had always hated lethargy, a testament to her immigrant mother.

From childhood, Eve's mother, Iwona, had drilled it into her that there was no time to lose: "We need work, food, beds, pots and pans, love. You think all this is going to fall in your lap? Go study." Iwona herself was always busy and grew restless if she had a free moment. She wouldn't sit still in one place. In the small apartment they lived in with squeaking floorboards, the sound of Iwona pacing the floor permeated the walls. She systematically and gradually discarded everything that stood in the way of her aspirations. Everything was disposable: names (Iwona became Yvonne and Ewa, Eve), accents, personal history. Yvonne was a pale, tubercular-looking woman with liquid blue eyes and lips that became visible only with lipstick. While Eve was still a baby, Yvonne attended secretarial school, and replaced her flat Polish locution with a lilting French accent. She made herself essential to the board members of Raft, Millenieux, and

Raft, an investment bank in Minneapolis where she worked as a secretary. Her typing speed of 140 words a minute was indispensable, but her alluring looks had an even greater value. When she came home from work, she would quickly clean her face and lips with cold cream, and change into a seersucker housecoat. After she plaited her hair, she would stride into the kitchen to prepare dinner. "What a day I've had," she'd tell Eve, who could be found sitting at the dinette table, wedged in the corner, doing homework.

On days when Eve's father worked late at the bakery, Yvonne and Eve would eat together. Crossing her arms across her body, her elbows planted on the vinyl tablecloth of daisies and bluebells, Yvonne would tell Eve about the way rich people dressed (in the palest of colors and natural fabrics), and how they held their wine goblets (by the stem) and their bodies (leaning back with ease, yet standing up to their true height), and how they spoke (softly and infrequently, so that everything they said seemed important). Yvonne would trace her fingers over her lips as she told her stories. Eve would stare at her plate when her mother did that.

"The Ambassador would like you in the Jade Room by seven," Lucy Ferguson, Andrew's secretary said, proffering a forced, pinched smile. It was the Empty Hour, and Eve was lying on the couch holding an ice pack to her forehead. She was wearing a *pareo* halter-style over her customary black swimsuit. The pareo split in two, from her abdomen down to her knees, showing pale skin slack with age, and ashy from the heat. Her toenails were unpainted, broken, thin. A five-toed sloth, Lucy thought. "The Ambassador would like you to dress modestly," Lucy said, even though the Ambassador had said no such thing. She was holding a small portfolio against her chest with both hands crossed over it in an X. "We are hosting some rising stars on the local political scene."

"I don't feel up to it," Eve said. Her eyes were closed.

"The Ambassador's wife has certain duties," Lucy said, coldly.

"What would be the loss if I didn't attend?"

Lucy, aware that she might explode if she stayed any longer, left the room.

Lucy considered herself a right-thinking American. She believed in Jeffersonian democracy and the city on the hill. She thought of Americans as larger than life (she herself was over six feet tall), heroic, and full of expertise that could be harnessed to make the world a better place. She thought Eve despicable; she had the evidence. Instead of exuding American confidence and goodwill, instead of being a proper consort to the Ambassador, instead of attending luncheons and teas, giving speeches at Rotary club meetings, visiting hospitals, and showing up for dinners at the Embassy, Eve shut herself off in a private world.

From her office on the second floor of the Embassy next door, Lucy had a full view of the Ambassador's wife under the arches of the verandah behind the bungalow. Every day, while other diplomats' wives were out and about for one charity or another, Eve lounged on a chair under the arches, in her Esther Williams swimsuit, and a large, floppy straw hat that covered most of her face. There she whiled away the morning hours, drinking cold vodka cut with sweet vermouth, smoking cigarettes, and reading Henry James' novels: *The Bostonians*, *Washington Square*, *The American*. Several times, Lucy had seen Eve throw a towel over her stomach and legs and place her hands under the towel. Filthy woman! The Ambassador was a handsome, lusty man; there was no excuse. Lucy knew that as an American she had to set an example so that others could follow. When there were parties and dinners at the embassy, Lucy noted Eve's ten-minute appearances. If there were events at another embassy,

Eve pleaded for understanding of her nerves and her migraine headaches.

"I tried," Eve said, after she heard the door close behind Lucy. Her life with Andrew had been full of promise. Before their wedding, surprised and perhaps emboldened by her acceptance, for she was beautiful and he was not, Andrew had promised her that she would one day be at his side as he was sworn in as Ambassador to the Court of St. James, or perhaps to Paris, or Rome. To Eve, who had thought Andrew a dull bureaucrat—he researched and wrote reports on foreign countries and their goodwill towards American interests for the State Department—his intention came as a surprise. Though she had always thought him eminently suitable for the peaceful marriage she desired, it was the vastness of his ambition that offered her the promise of renewal.

Peace was important to Eve, as she had been dragged up by a father, who thrived on war, and died of cancer when she was nine. Thoughts of him, fleeting as they were, came to her now only when she walked past the tall china cabinets in the Embassy kitchen, filled with elegant dishes, bowls, and stemware for every spirit and wine. A thick-necked, hulking man, Jarek had bulging eyes and an angry nose. He worked as a waiter at a Polish bakery and café. "Woman's work," he ritually complained. On good days, he came home with things for the house: a crock pot, a toaster, a radio, and sat for dinner with Eve and her mother, his eyes glazed and shiny, delighted with his talent for hustling and stealing. "Today a free toaster, tomorrow a free television," he'd say, proud as proud can be. Ewa, Eve, was still young enough to be impressed, but Yvonne remained unmoved, casting her eyes down, cutting her food with short grating sounds, clamping her dead lips between bites. Other days, Jarek stormed through the apartment, a black look on his face, nostrils flaring. He would rush past Eve into the kitchen and open and shut the cabinet doors. Eve would hear his canvas shoes grate and squeak against the hardwood floor, which buckled from age and neglect. Jarek would prowl from room to room, shouting Yvonne's other name. "How much are you hiding from me? What are you hiding from me?" he'd shout as he hurled dishes and plates at Yvonne, but always falling short, the noise of shattering plates permeating the walls. Yvonne, wily and fast, would climb out the window and down the fire escape to safety. Jarek was left to simmer down. "Just watch the TV, this is all you have to do," he would say in a low voice, as he sat on the couch and pulled Eve onto his lap. She knew she had to stay quiet until the hardness under his clothes became soft, and the wetness seeped through his clothes onto her skirt. "How you calm me with this small gift," he would whisper against her cheek. She wanted peace in their lives; it was easy to leave her body.

Jarek had a long, drawn-out death in the free ward of the local hospital. Yvonne, who had endured his anger and hoped to see a conversion brought on by the pain and fathoming of his own mortality, was disappointed. She had hoped for some humility in her abusive husband, some sign of regret, some words of sorrow, a plea to her for forgiveness for the wrong he had done her. But that was not to be. He was more demonic as he lay dying than before his body conspired against him. Once, as she'd tried to prop his pillows because there was nothing else she could do for him, he'd grunted, "Get me the nurse, you whore."

"Is he going to die?" Eve had asked her mother that day as they waited outside the hospital gates for the bus to take them home.

"As it pleases God."

After Jarek's death, Yvonne moved herself and her daughter to a neat duplex closer the bank, so that she could devote herself to her work without worrying about missing the last train home. She earned enough to give Eve a fine education: private school, piano, ballet, etiquette, and elocution lessons when young, and a degree in art history from a fine college in the East, all out of an unspecified guilt. "Marry an intellectual," she told Eve. When Eve brought home Andrew Mallon, bearer of a law degree from Yale, a doctorate in Political Science from Harvard, and a recent graduate of the Foreign Services Institute, Yvonne marveled at her own good luck. In the end, all pain is rewarded, she thought. "An Ambassadorship is a possibility?" Yvonne asked the young man.

"I have a good to great shot of establishing myself at the Court of Saint James," he replied.

That was eighteen years ago.

Andrew had been visa officer in Delhi, third secretary at the consulate in Jamaica, cultural affairs secretary at the embassy in Rhodesia, programs officer at the consulate in Turkey, and Deputy Consul General in Nigeria. Then he was nominated Ambassador to Chomumbhar. Eve cried when she first heard the news. She had a perfect wardrobe for London, Rome, Paris, Berlin, and Vienna, even. She had a Jean Patou gown so stunning, if ever a high level authority had insisted she take part in a *passagiato* in Rome, she would have been the toast of that city. She had a Lanvin perfect for Covent Garden, a Balenciaga designed by the great man himself, and a milliner with dreams of turning heads at Ascot. She had counted on erasure and disremembering. But some part of Eve was still in that house in Minnesota, with its squeaky floorboards buckled from sin and sorrow. She could not conjure up an amnesia that would allow her to move on.

The Quiet American Speaks

I had been in the Far East exactly six months when the Colonel called me from his desk at Langley. He asked if I would brief some visiting senators on Third Force Democracy, the use of subsidized paramilitary forces to install democracy in places threatened by communism.

"I just did. They were just here," I yelled into the telephone at the Economic Aid Mission where I worked. Even from the specially equipped secure telephones at the Legation, international calls in those days were full of static, crackles, whistles, and echoes. I heard my words reach Virginia and circle back to Saigon three seconds after I had emitted them. *I I just just did did they they were were just just here here.*

"Armed Forces persuaded. Hammer Foreign Relations," the Colonel said.

I understood the Colonel to mean that the Senate Armed Forces Committee had been impressed by my lecture, and that he wanted me to repeat my performance to the Foreign Relations Committee.

It had taken me many months to understand the Colonel's truncated, disjointed manner of speaking. His staccato pronouncements were bones absent of marrow, sentences devoid of flourish: evil punish, duty kill, America mighty. He used forceful verbs—persuade, brief, hammer, strike, decapitate, annihilate—to motivate those under his command. At first, I had thought his delivery bizarre, but I soon came to realize that his condensed sentences, usually limited to nouns and verbs, were managerial directives, pre-emptive strikes against discussion and consensus.

The Colonel had never disclosed his grand ambition or vision for Indochina in detail. Perhaps he would have sounded excessive if he had said freedom and democracy were the Almighty's gift to every man and woman in the world, and that as the greatest power on the face of the earth, America had an obligation to help its expansion. Perhaps there would have been those who questioned the grandiosity of such a declaration. Instead, the Colonel's simple ejaculations cloaked his messianic impulse and rendered his schemes practical and reasonable.

"Support imperative," the Colonel said.

The Colonel was absolute in his thinking and free from doubt. He liked ideas best when they could be reduced to one word. The Colonel believed in America, Democracy, Freedom, Supremacy, Capitalism, Resolve, Honor, and Courage, words he always capitalized in his memos, because, he said, they ennobled the human spirit. At the same time, the Colonel violently opposed other one-word ideas: communism, socialism, nationalism, autonomy, independence, doubt, and nuance, always in lowercase. Sometimes, when the Colonel was especially buoyant and lucid, he would articulate ideas that he had fused together from his circumscribed lexicon: communism evil, dictator mad, America Right, Democracy Good.

I believed in the same ideas. I believed my country had a moral responsibility to thwart communism and assist emerging nations set up the infrastructures for Freedom, Peace, and Prosperity. Deep down, I knew that all people dreamed American dreams of self-actualization. However, my deeply held beliefs about bringing democracy to emerging nations were not very popular in Saigon, especially among the expatriates. Thomas Fowler, an Englishman and a correspondent for *The London Times*, took particular issue with my ideas.

"Vietnam, an emerging nation? Do you mean compared to Hawaii, New Mexico, and Puerto Rico?" he asked.

He was always mocking my country, my values, me.

"Do you think that a peasant thinks of God and democracy when he gets inside his mud hut at night?" he asked.

"Yes!" I said. Thomas just didn't understand. He was the most cynical, disillusioned man I had ever met. He believed in nothing.

Individual lives could be turned around because of Democracy, and ruined by something as mundane as apathy. I had seen it myself. I had seen Democracy in action, the way it had saved Phuong and her sister, Miss Hei. Thanks to our well-funded mission in Saigon, Miss Hei was working as a secretary at the American Legation, and making an envious living by her own people's standards. And Phuong was better off for having left Thomas, and accepting my care and protection.

"Briefing necessary," the Colonel said.

"With all due respect, Sir, General The and I are in the middle of organizing the second phase of our campaign," I said.

American public opinion on Indochina had been eroding for months, because of the increasing number of flag-draped coffins turning up at Dover. We needed to turn things around. We were planning a spectacular event on *rue Catinat* that would look like a Viet Minh bombing. The's militia would carry it out. One of the goals was to pave the way for us to install our man, General Ngo Din Diem in power. Diem was no saint but he understood what was expected of him. He may be a son of a bitch, the Colonel had said, but he's our son of a bitch. Diem was cooling his heels back in suburban New Jersey while we worked to create a leadership vacuum in Indochina. The previous month, we had filled bicycle pumps with plastic bombs and set them off all over Saigon. I told the Colonel I needed more Dialacton, the plastic we used for the bombs.

"Much more warranted, additional threat," the Colonel said. "Another Third Force needed."

I didn't respond. I was unaware of any other Communist regimes in South Asia.

" Chomumbhar," the Colonel said.

My sigh sounded like a truck roar because of the double echo vaulting through the telephone lines. It took all I had to keep up with what was going on in Indochina.

I knew York Harding's books and theories on the region inside out, but it had been over two years since York had been to the place himself. Much of what I knew was outdated by the time I had arrived in Asia. A lot had changed since York wrote *The Advance of Red China*.

It was fortunate that I met Thomas my very first week in Saigon. He was sitting at one of the small café tables at the bar of the Continental, on *rue Catinat*. I was walking across the square, feeling light in my head and heavy on my feet. I was still suffering from jetlag, and I had trouble breathing because of the humidity. I could feel the sweat on the back of my thighs trickling down my legs and pooling in the back of my knees. I needed a cold beer to revive me. I didn't see a free table on the sidewalk, so I headed towards one that was occupied by a lone man.

"Do you mind?" I asked the man, and sat down before he could say yes.

Thomas admired the girls. "They are lovely, aren't they?" he asked, as the women walked by, clad in colorful *ao dai*—silk tunics with slits at the sides, and white silk trousers.

"Sure," I agreed.

Thomas filled me in on developments in Saigon. In Tonkin, the French were just barely hanging on to the Red River delta. The Viet Minh could win if the Chinese allied with them against the French. And that was just in the north. In the south, Thomas said the French controlled the main roads until seven. Then there were the Caodaists, the Hoa-Haos, and the Binh Xuyen, he said.

* * *

"What's your thesis, Colonel?" I asked.

"Piss pot south of India west of Australia. Sorry-assed dictator," the Colonel said. "Take him out."

I knew where Chomumbhar was, sort of, and the General did not mean it the way it sounded. What he meant was that he wanted to reclaim Chomumbhar for Democracy, and bring American-imposed order to it.

The Colonel saw us Americans as noble warriors, who would turn nations from tyranny to Democracy. I did not think in such majestic terms, but I knew we were good and decent, and wanted only the best for the world. Democracy was essential to the greater good. I knew this. I felt it. According to the Colonel, the government of Chomumbhar, led by its Prime Minister, Ferdinand D'Souza, had failed to uphold American ideals and values. "Human rights non-existent," the Colonel said. I felt a little uneasy with that statement since our own Negro question, with a spate of lynchings that month alone, left a great deal to be desired. The Colonel was adamant. He wanted to push for a Third Force there, similar to the actions we were taking in Indochina. He wanted me to fly to our embassy in Bangkok and brief a group of visiting senators on Harding's principles. I was reluctant about traveling anywhere right then. I didn't think we could afford to wage war on a second front, for one thing.

For another, Phuong had just moved in with me. I had won her by default; she had left Thomas because he had lied to her, not because she loved me. She hadn't brought all her things to my flat near *rue Durantot*. Only two of her *ao dai* were hanging in the wardrobe. In the drawer next to mine, she kept her colorful silk scarves and three pairs of culottes. Under the bed, she kept a box with her only reading, "*The Pictorial Life of the Royal Family.*" She had not seemed like someone ready to share a life.

Thomas told me her name meant "phoenix" in Vietnamese. I thought sometimes that she was like a caged bird, just waiting to fly away. I had to be careful not to take her for granted.

She had not forgotten Thomas, I knew. Several times since she had begun to live with me, she had begun speaking in French—the way she would have with Thomas. She had come home from the movies one day, and I asked her about it in English.

"How did it go?"

"Go?" she asked vacantly.

"The movie?"

"Le film?"

"Yes, the film."

"Etait tres triste," she said *"L'amour n'a pas duré."*

"Hold your horses, slow down," I said. My French was very bad, and I had insisted from the beginning that she speak only English with me.

"Je crois que c'était une grande erreur dans l'histoire."

"It's inconsiderate of you to speak so fast," I scolded her.

"Comment?"

"You're thinking of him, aren't you?"

She looked at me blankly.

"Thomas?"

"Fowlair?" She cast her eyes down. Beautiful, inscrutable, unknowable woman.

"Fowler. Yes," I corrected her, enunciating both syllables, as if I were speaking to a child.

"No," she said. And then, *"Est ce que je peux te préparer un bol d'opium?"*

That made me very angry, as I did not smoke anything, least of all opium.

It was a terrible, immoral thing. Thomas smoked at least a dozen pipes a day. I feel sure it contributed to his moral lapses. The women supported the habit; they believed that their foreign lovers would always come back if they smoked. A terrible thing. It would have been a bad time for me to leave Phuong, before she had learned to think of me first.

"I wish you would assign someone else, Colonel," I said. I

was also reluctant to leave so close to the big campaign. "There is to be a parade," I said.

"Logistics to follow," he said, and hung up.

I knocked on Joe's office door and walked in. Miss Hei, Phuong's sister, was sitting on a parson's chair, her back straight, a small chignon caught in a black hair net. She was wearing a purple *ao dai* with white silk trousers. Though she had a trim, neat figure, she did not wear her clothes like her sister. Miss Hei was an efficient woman, meant to work for a living; she was hard and unbreakable, unlike Phuong, who was beautiful, the most beautiful woman in all Saigon, and so innocent. Miss Hei was taking notes while Joe paced the room and dictated a letter.

Joe looked at me distractedly and resumed his pacing. "No, scratch that," he told Miss Hei. She stared at me as she waited for Joe's dictation.

"The Colonel wants me to go to Bangkok to brief a visiting delegation."

"Yes. Senate Foreign Relations," Joe said.

"What about the plans in the works?" I was deliberately vague, since I could not be sure that Miss Hei was loyal to our cause.

"It's only for the weekend. We'll manage without you," Joe said.

I flew in and out of Bangkok without incident. I had prepared myself for the presentation by re-reading the entire works of York Harding: *The Advance of Red China*, *The Challenge to Democracy*, *The Role of the West*. The briefing was successful: the senators listened, took copious notes, and thanked me at the end for my insights.

I returned to Saigon, and was surprised and happy to see a change in Phuong. I think she had reconciled some things to herself while I had been gone. Perhaps she finally understood that her future lay with me. She did not read or write like her sister, which eliminated the possibility of a respectable job. I think Phuong realized that without me, and with Thomas unavailable, she could easily have ended up with someone vile like Granger. Without a man, she must have known that she would end up like those young women at the House of Five Hundred Girls. In her face then, I saw none of the doubt I had seen before. She seemed to have made a decision—to let me save her.

We sat at an outdoor table at the Continental and ate lunch. Duke, my chow, sat at her feet and watched her with his liquid eyes. He occasionally licked her hand with his black tongue. I looked at her through the aperture of a camera I had bought in Bangkok. Beautiful, inscrutable, unknowable woman.

After lunch, we walked towards the botanical gardens. A swarm of rickshaws stood idle outside the entrance while their owners napped under the palm trees. When we stopped in front of a large stone dragon, Phuong shoved my camera at a rickshaw puller, and asked him to take a picture of us. He turned his back to me as he listened to Phuong explain the camera's workings. He wore a stained yellow singlet and long pants rolled up above the knees. His legs were sturdy like tree trunks, tight and bulging at the calves, the blue veins criss-crossing the back of his legs like a map. She circled the man and came back to me. She took Duke's leash from me, and leaned her beautiful, bird-like body against mine. Her silky, jet-black hair brushed my shoulders.

I thought of the work that lay ahead of me, to bring Democracy and Freedom at any cost to the people of Indochina and Chomumbhar. I would need a lot more Dialacton. At that moment, I felt everything was going right with me.

ISLAND MAIL REVIEW

PM writes national poem "Pearl Of My Eye." Urges citizens to memorize it.

Lady Lalitha planning new childcare initiative. Tells women to work for money and save for old age.

Star high school students to receive awards from PM. Poor performers told to prepare for mediocre lives.

Ban on kissing and necking at botanical gardens. This is not Europe, public areas not your bedroom, PM says.

More Live With Heartbreak

(1970s – 1980s)

ISLAND MAIL REVIEW

PM plays golf with Australian delegation. Not happy with performance. Hires coach, fires caddy.

Lady Lalitha complains of citizenry's sloppy dressing. "Ugly and poor people should try harder." Institutes dress code.

PM tells students headed for World Math Olympics to win.

U.S. Ambassador and female diplomat spotted at Gelinta Highlands.

Ambassador's wife critical after rescue from accident wreckage. Apparent suicide motive.

Court of No Appeal

Soly Ashani, Chief Magistrate of the Civic Court in the Republic of Chomumbhar, woke one June day to the usual chirp of mynah and drongo birds, and an unfamiliar constriction in his chest. It was not a heart attack, he was certain. He had poured a lifetime of care and devotion on his fifty-seven-year-old body. No meat had ever defiled it. He had practiced ayurveda, kriya yoga, and kundalini for well nigh twenty years. He neither drank nor smoked. He minded his chakras. He slept only as much as he needed to and no more. He walked, cycled, and swam every day. He had no family to speak of. In short, Soly had done everything imaginable to avoid the possibility of a shriveled life—illness, degeneration, encumbrances.

"Soly" was an abbreviation for "Solina." But as soon as the island's Ministry of Culture had appointed him to preside over its recently formed Civic Court, Soly gave himself a new name—one more in keeping with his role as the leading arbiter of civic justice in the Republic of Chomumbhar.

The day Soly received his letter of appointment, he visited Kowloon Printers in Port Contadu (their motto: "Here Got Engraving"), and ordered new business cards printed on their finest ivory stock. The raised-edge lettering read: Solomon Ashani, LLB, J.D, Chief Magistrate, Civic Court, Ministry of Culture of the Republic of Chomumbhar.

Soly's job as chief magistrate was a significant promotion from his last position as senior barrister at the Board of Water Works. Though that agency had insisted on LL.B. and J.D degrees – both of which Soly possessed – the work demanded little in the way of judicial maneuverings. The threat of dry taps and the nominal annual fee of 12 *flores* guaranteed timely payment by all water consumers. There was no occasion for him to write pleadings or briefs, to take depositions, or file motions. There was little call for Soly to orchestrate shrewd legal chess games, and none at all to make court appearances. This was a particular regret, since Soly believed that he had been blessed with a conspicuous eloquence. He was, after all, a Rahmin.

"Aryan blood courses through our veins," his mother had reminded him from the time he was a boy. She told him he was superior—intended for great things. He drank the notion like first milk. Through his twenties and thirties, matchmakers approached Soly's widowed mother, bringing word of suitable Rahmin brides and large dowries. "She won't suit us," Soly's mother had said, dismissing every offer. The woman in question was too dark, too simple, too cunning, too humble, too arrogant, too religious, too hedonistic. "Remember who you are," she said of his Aryan bloodlines.

She convinced him. He remained unshaken in his belief that a Rahmin woman meriting his love and attention was his destiny. He didn't mind waiting. And while he waited, he frequented the prostitution dens outside the U.S. Military base in Riyalh. As a Rahmin, he was bound by tradition not to contaminate himself, but sixty *flores* would buy him quick relief from deft-handed women wearing ribbed latex gloves. He brought the gloves.

When he heard of accomplished Rahmin men of his acquaintance marrying commoners, thinning the blood, he felt an instant loss of respect for them. He stopped socializing with friends who had gone abroad to British and American universities and returned with foreign wives. "My reputation is in shreds, thanks to you," he scolded his cousin, Rei, who had returned from England with a Jamaican woman he had met in medical school. "You should have seen her hair," Soly said, trying to describe an Afro to his mother. There was little Soly shared with his mother anymore, other than a violent objection to anyone not Rahmin.

A year after he had joined the Board of Water Works, Soly knew that he had squandered his talents. Nevertheless, he remained at the department for more than two decades. As the years passed, Soly's ambitions became soft, like dough, and he began to forget that he had once meant to make a mark, a grand flourish with his life. It ceased to matter. The salary he drew from the agency was sufficient for his needs, few as they were.

On his way home from work each day, Soly would stop at Change Alley for his evening meal. Over the years, Soly noticed that even the stall owners, poor and illiterate as they were, enjoyed companionship, solidarity with others. They had wives, children, kin, while he, Soly, stood alone, embalmed in sarcasm and regret. One stall owner, Anan, a cheerful but lowly Rahmin, was especially galling to Soly. At first, Soly had been impressed with Anan for a singular reason: that he always washed his hands before preparing Soly's chapatis. Later, through his daily visits to Change Alley, Soly met Anan's wife, Muni, whom he had married with great fanfare.

She had been the last Qalit to be branded in Chomumbhar. Soly objected to the notoriety and fame she had earned for defying the race laws. As a child, she had crashed a garden party at *Flore de la Mar* hosted by the Prime Minister and First Lady. The Health Minister, who had been drinking a great deal at the soirée, passed on his suspicions to Lady Lalitha, who promptly ejected Muni from the grounds.

After the Kennedys had left for India, some stragglers from the foreign press had learned about the incident, reported it over the wires, and made it an international incident. A diplomatic furor had ensued. Port Contadu and Washington engaged in lengthy negotiations. Lady Lalitha stood her ground; she pleaded for foreigners to be mindful of Chomumbhar's history, culture, religions, and mores.

The American Ambassador informed the Prime Minister that the President and Mrs. Kennedy viewed Chomumbhar as a progressive nation, and were deeply disappointed by the Qalit laws.

"And how about your race problems, Mr. Ambassador? Are you not hanging black people from trees?" Lady Lalitha asked.

"That is beside the point," said the Ambassador.

The President sent a telegram asking the Prime Minister to reconsider. "The whole world is watching. By this single act, you will put your island on the map of great nations."

Mrs. Kennedy placed a personal call to Lady Lalitha. The architect of the Qalit laws relented. "One was unable to ever say no to them," Lady Lalitha would later remark.

The Prime Minister agreed to repeal the laws of Untouchability and end the practice of branding, as part of a reciprocal agreement. The Americans promptly rewarded Chomumbhar with the airline Lady Lalitha had long desired. A fleet of four Douglas DC3s, three Boeing 707s, and three 727s was dispatched to the island for the launch of Chomumbhar Airways—a gift from the American people. In addition, Mrs. Kennedy assigned her personal couturier, Oleg Cassini, to design the flight crew uniforms. You will have seen the sepia-toned advertisements of Chomumbhar Airways on television, the smiling, sarong clad 'Chomumbhar Girl' inviting you to "the island of pearls and dreams."

Anan and Muni had two children, Karo and Jahn, named in honor of the Kennedy children.

Soly had watched the pair as they raised their mongrel children behind the gas burners and frying pans. By the time eighteen years had gone by, and Soly had buried both his parents, Anan and Muni had earned enough money to send Jahn to medical school in India and, two years later, Karo to nursing school in Philippines. Soly saw in Anan's and Muni's life, progress, pitch, tilt, addition, multiplication, change as sure as the monsoon.

"Where is my reward? My wife? My son? My daughter?" Soly raged bitterly, silently.

For Soly then, the job of Chief Magistrate was his second chance— his reinvented *karma*. He felt that the circumstances were the Creator's way of repairing his, he hated to admit it, shriveled life. Soly now set off for a work in a chauffeured sedan assigned by the Ministry.

The Civic Court was housed in magnificent quarters, a stone and marble palace of Moorish design. Each façade of the building had grand double-arched entryways, the tops embellished with pierced stone filigree. Minarets of white and gray marble, sprouting overblown bulbs, adorned the four corners of the roof. A turbaned, khaki-clad soldier, with a baton belted to his hip and a Kalishnokov hanging from a shoulder, stood at the entrance of the red-bricked building. Each day, he greeted Soly with sniveling bows and multiple, "Your Honors."

In the cavernous, domed lobby, the Ministry's canon of edicts were depicted and illustrated on large theater posters with such titles as *Five Fingers of Justice, Proper Behaviors, Good Citizenship*, and *Right Thinking*. In the middle of the lobby, near a gurgling fountain under the skylights, paralegals sat on canvas folding chairs behind school desks bearing ancient Olivetti and Brother typewriters. Clusters and chains of people swarmed around the paralegals for legal assistance. Since nearly everything was a crime in Chomumbhar, there were long waits for the paralegals' services.

Soly would often linger in the lobby, enjoying the motions of justice at the lowest level, before he ascended the winding marble staircase to his own venerable station.

Soly's photographic memory had allowed him to

memorize by heart the laws of Chomumbhar that multiplied with each passing month. The penalties for violating the laws of the land were crafted and handed down by Prime Minister Ferdinand D'Souza himself. The PM was prolific and specific. In memos marked "Prime Minister's 20/20 Vision Plan," Soly was informed of new edicts, new laws, and new infractions to punish:

- Unruly behavior and hooliganism by males – 1,500 *flores* fine;
- Unruly behavior and hooliganism by females - 1,500 *flores* fine and mandatory participation by errant female in "Womanly Conduct" seminars;
- Immodest and provocative attire (both sexes) – confiscation of offending garments and fine of 2,000 *flores*;
- Second pregnancy – fine of 5,000 *flores* and dispatch of errant couple to Ministry of Culture's rehabilitation program;
- Third and succeeding pregnancies – enlistment of errant couple in the "Zero and Right Population Growth" program;
- Divorce for any reason – communal shunning of entire family unit;
- Homosexuality, bisexuality, and transvestitism – thirty lashes with bamboo cane.

Soly loved stepping into his chambers—grand rooms and anterooms lined in dark wood paneling. From the vestibule, he could look directly into his office. He always made a point of casting a sweeping gaze over the entire east wall of shelves holding legal volumes, which anchored his muscular teak desk. A chaise stood against the west wall. A door near the chaise led to a small bathroom, and an anteroom that Soly used to store the PM's now obsolete legal declarations and renderings. Flanking the main entry, a black lacquered wooden tree as tall as a man, to hold umbrellas, hats, and coats, held three identical magistrates' robes. A ledge protruding from the navel of the hall tree held twin white mannequin heads. Two identical, gray-haired wigs framed the foam shapes. Out of reverence for his office, Soly never ventured into his chambers without wearing one of the robes. Soly was pleased with the way he looked in the shiny, black shantung silks with generous swathes of fabric falling in drapes at the shoulders, the edges piped in deep vermilion brocade.

During his first week as magistrate, in addition to wearing his robe, Soly also donned one of the wigs before entering his chambers. It was a vanity. He was required to wear the ceremonial accessory only while performing his duties at the bench. Soly would hook his thumbs into the small slits at the sides of his robe and walk around his desk feeling powerful and wise. "The law is reason free of passion," he would intone to his library of books. "The very law which molds a tear and bids it trickle from its source—that law preserves the earth a sphere and guides the planets to their course." He would recite Aristotle and Homer, Hammurabi and Swift, as he circled his desk in his elegant wig. He found the heat in the chambers intolerable that first week. Despite the ceiling fan churning and whipping the air in the rooms, Soly was compelled to lift the wig to scratch his bald head and wipe the sweat off it. After that, he wore his wig only when court was in session.

Soly's law clerk, Kamila, usually knocked on the door around eight each morning. She would place the day's case roster on a tiered basket perched on Soly's desk. He had only recently begun to enjoy her visits. The first time he had set eyes on Kamila, he thought her ugly beyond redemption. He suspected her of being a Qalit. How else to explain her squat figure, or her roughly hewn features, or that chin jutting out in simian fashion? The shapeless black smock she was required to wear as a junior law clerk flattered her not at all. Your looks do not serve you well and more is the pity, Soly thought as he dismissed her. But truth changes every day, doesn't it? A few months after working with Kamila, Soly noted that she wore no ring on her finger though she was well past her prime. He revised his opinion of her. She and I are alike, Soly decided. Nobody waited for us; nobody found us. You can weave love out of almost anything, if you feel it in your loins first. He settled the matter to himself.

First, he brought her candies and sweets. She thanked him, but her eyebrows arched in surprise, her lips pursed in a tight hole as if she were containing her mirth, laughing at him, he was sure of it. Then he invited her to lunch. She refused, claiming she was busy. He asked her again several times. She refused each time: "Very kind of you, but—," she'd say, swinging her typist chair, crossing her hefty legs, picking up the telephone, and punching the numbers on the pad with a pencil. Then he gave her books of poetry, Rumi, Neruda, Scheherazade, until he had nothing else to give her. She mumbled and smiled her thanks (her smiles no longer reached her eyes), and added them to the steadily growing pile on the floor behind her desk. It hurt Soly to see his beloved poems lying there, neglected, forgotten. He wanted Kamila to be grateful to him, Solomon Ashani, LLB, JD, Chief Magistrate, for waiting for her.

The pain in his chest grew worse that June day. He spent the morning stroking and massaging the knot of strained muscles. Kamila knocked on his door and entered without waiting for him to admit her.

"I'm indisposed," Soly said, leaning forward to plant his elbows on his desk, his open palms crossed and resting on his shoulders. The fluorescent lights threw iridescent greens and purples off his bald head.

"Shouldn't your honor be apprised?" Kamila waited for Soly to pick up the case roster she had placed in his basket earlier.

"Alright," Soly sighed. He uncrossed his hands and brought them to the table. He read the first case on the roster. He looked up at Kamila. "Why does the Ministry insist on prosecuting this bloody nonsense?"

Kamila shrugged.

Was it just Soly's imagination or had she grown more beautiful? "Let's get on with the second, State versus Valladares," Soly said.

"Violating the sanctity of womanhood, Your Honor," Kamila's mouth twitched at the corners in a smile.

Soly loved the lipstick she had deemed to wear that day. It was not shiny, but sealed her lips in a dry coat of pomegranate—the color of her vagina, probably, he thought.

"In what manner?" He stroked his own bottom lip with the pad of his index finger. It felt like a kiss. *I love her; I am nothing without her*, the thoughts burrowed into him. Soly imagined a naked Kamila on her back, sprawled across his desk. He saw himself running his hand up and down the length of her stocky leg.

"Opinionated and proud, Your Honor." She thrust her enormous jaw up, and clicked her tongue to emphasize the absurdity of the charge.

"Any witnesses for the prosecution?" Soly blinked to erase the image of his law clerk naked, spread-eagled across his desk.

"The mother-in-law, Your Honor."

"Very well. That will be all." He wanted to ask her to accompany him to Change Alley for lunch, but he didn't think he could stand another careless rejection.

Instead, he locked the door after her, lay down on the chaise, reached under his robe and trousers, and worked the stem of his erection until he ejaculated. The pain in his chest receded. He washed his hands and face at the bathroom sink, and brushed his moustache with the ivory comb he always kept in his shirt pocket. He slipped out through a side door from the anteroom of his chambers, and went to Anan's stall for lunch.

Anan was sick and had gone to see his son, Muni informed him. "My son, the doctor," Muni said, proudly.

"Who's doing the cooking, then?" Soly asked.

"Making chapatis is not brain surgery, Mr. Chief Magistrate," Muni said, tying an apron around her waist. "Onion or no?"

Soly looked at the marks on her hand as she rolled the chapati dough vigorously and pummeled it. It's the end of civilization, he thought, as his lips curled down in protest.

"You think I will contaminate your food, Mr. Soly?"

"Ah, no," he said awkwardly, surprised by her impudence.

"Sit down, your Royal Highness," she said, dropping ghee on the griddle.

Soly turned and walked towards a table.

"The man who thinks he shits gold, eats alone," she muttered over the sizzle of the ghee.

He needed to eat. What else could he do? He sat down.

"I promise I won't breathe on it," she shouted after him. "Only spit in it, as usual."

Soly sat down at a table and glowered at Muni. He regretted the loss of certainty, the assurance that had cloaked him like soft cashmere when everything was nailed to its proper place. The world was changing at a furious pace around him, spinning, spinning, leaving him unhinged and bitter.

An hour later, Soly admitted himself to his chambers and cast his customary sweep over his wall of books. The pain in his chest was worse; he felt he had violated a holy thing by eating from the hand of an Untouchable. The door to his archives was ajar. Strange, he thought, as he walked towards it.

Kamila was sitting on the edge of a low file cabinet, her legs wrapped around the turbaned guard. Her hands cupped the guard's buttocks. They were both fully clothed, but the lewdness of the pairing stung Soly like a colony of bees. Soly stepped back, grabbed his robe and wig, and retreated through the main door.

The court looked less like a court than it did a church. An aisle running down the length of the room separated the pews, just like at church. At the head of the pews, the prosecution sat on upholstered, high-backed chairs behind a long wood table. There was no similar seating for the defense. Simply put, there was no defense. The judge's dais stood on a raised platform at the front of the room; the seal of the republic emblazoned the dais. A shorter podium was situated to the right of the judge's lectern.

"The Honorable Solomon Ashani, Presiding Magistrate. All rise," the bailiff intoned.

Soly massaged his chest under his robe as he climbed the short stack of stairs leading to his bench.

"The State versus A. Morais," the bailiff shouted with gusto.

Soly could not understand why the bailiff executed such loud emissions in a closed court. After all, there were only five people in the room.

Morais was sworn in before he took the stand. The prosecutor for the Ministry of Culture, a man with a penguin shape wearing a black robe with a white shirt peeking from under it, stood up and adjusted his wig.

"What happened on June eighth?" Soly asked the penguin.

"On the night in question, Your Honor, the defendant repeatedly blasted on his stereo the song, 'Strangers in the Night' by Frank Sinatra."

"And what of it?" Soly asked.

"The Ministry maintains, Your Honor, that the words of the aforementioned song violate the Decency Act and promote decadent living, one night stands, adultery, rape, venereal diseases, and unwanted pregnancy."

"Was he with someone?"

"Yes, Your Honor. The errant female has been dispatched for rehabilitation. She was morally challenged, Your Hon—"

"—Spare me your prejudice and get on with your case," Soly interrupted.

"Very well, Your Honor," said the penguin. "In the Asian context, specifically in the context of our island's culture, Your Honor, the words of this song violate all our national values, indeed everything we stand for. The Ministry maintains that it is immoral and perverse, Your Honor, 'for strangers in the night to exchange glances and hope for love before the night is through'."

"Are there any witnesses?" Soly asked.

"No, Your Honor. The prosecution rests its case," the penguin said.

"The defendant, please rise!" the bailiff yelled.

Mr. A. Morais stood up.

"Do you have anything to say in your own defense, Mr. Morais?" Soly asked, with a compassionate tilt of his head.

"Yes, Your Honor," the man said gravely.

Soly appreciated remorse. He leaned forward with Solomonic understanding. "I am all ears," he said.

"Where would this country be without a sorry bastard like you?" The defendant's mouth hardly moved, but Soly knew he had said it. The smirk on the man's face and the triumphal arch of his eyebrow proved his corrupt nature.

"The law is the true embodiment of everything that is excellent, Mr. Morais," Judge Solomon Ashani said in finding the defendant guilty.

The Apparition

It was mangosteen season when thirteen-year-old Maya Gomez vanished, and the green-eyed woman, Mariel Vega, appeared at the Cathedral of the Holy Comforter in Port Contadu. The crop was so plentiful that year that the lateral 'steen' branches, with their smooth, leathery leaves, bowed with the weight of ripe, unharvested fruit. Maya and Mariel worked at a bar in Riyalh, a city on the western coast of the main island. Maya was a hostess at *Hot Well*, Mariel, its singer and star attraction. Riyalh housed the largest U.S military installation in Asia.

Chomumbhar was an important tile in America's domino theory—essential for a stable and peaceful Near and Far East. On one side, military generals and teary-eyed widows of assassinated leaders ruled, plundered, and punished with the best of intentions. On the other, religious zealots ranted against Western decadence and US imperialism. India and Pakistan flexed their muscles at each other, and China and North Korea breathed the fire of stirring dragons. But the presence of fifty thousand American servicemen on the island gave us, the progeny of pearl divers, fishermen, and pacifists, a swaggering optimism. Who would attack us when armed American gladiators would crush them like a rolled-up newspaper whacking a tsetse fly?

Throughout history, we had looked to mercenaries and others to fight our wars. In 1540, under siege by Muslim pirates, Chomumbhar's governing elders dispatched an emissary to Goa to plead for Portuguese protection. The emissary returned with an armada of fifty vessels—frigates, galleons, and light galleys—

equipped with guns and whatnot, and a few thousand men. Francis Xavier, then preaching in Goa, blessed the flagship and the soldiers with his own holy hands. The Portuguese defeated the Muslims in six days. In return, the elders agreed to send three boatloads of pearls to Lisbon for the Queen's slippers, and to welcome Francis Xavier to the island. To make room for the pearls, the flotilla left behind some men, those who found the weather fine and the women beautiful. Maya and Mariel were the descendants of the soldiers from the flotilla.

It was the third week of mangosteen season when Maya disappeared. Split mangosteen shells, their pearly white segments intact, littered the island like spent bullet casings. In wealthy neighborhoods, Qalit street cleaners speared rogue mangosteens with long handled picks. In poor neighborhoods, like the one Maya's family lived in, people and animals feasted on the manna.

On Mondays, her day off, Maya would make the twenty-mile trek to Port Contadu by bus to visit her parents and to give them her pay. Maya's parents didn't worry when she failed to show up that third week of mangosteen season. They thought she had secured overtime to double her wages. But when she didn't return the following week as well, they went to Riyalh. *Deus Mae*—Godmother, the owner of *Hot Well,* told them their daughter had run away. The distraught parents rushed back to Port Contadu to see Father Daniel Sullivan, their parish priest at Holy Comforter. Father Daniel was an American Jesuit held in special regard by the islanders. He was a living link to their first encounter with faith—it was his Order's apostles who had first brought Christ to the island.

"I didn't think Maya was old enough to be in Riyalh," Father Daniel said, hurrying into the sunny parlor of the presbytery. Daniel had baptized Maya, confirmed her, and listened to her confession of childish sins: hitting my brother, calling my sister stupid, sticking my tongue out at mother, killing snails with salt. Daniel plopped down on a chair and stretched out his long legs. He was not wearing the brown robes of the Society of Jesus, or a cassock, or even the more conventional cleric's collar. Instead, he had on a colorful batik shirt, like the local men, paired with drab chinos and sandals.

"She is hostess, no different from air stewardess," Mr. Gomez said, fingering the lapels of his shirt, as he sat stiffly on the couch across from Daniel.

"The work is clean," Mrs. Gomez added, perched on the edge of the sofa next to her husband.

"I didn't know things were that bad," Daniel told Mr. Gomez. The pupils of his large blue eyes grew larger as the sun pooled around his chair.

"I'm squeezing a sorry living out of sand, Father. The oysters are no good. And the fish are worse," Mr. Gomez said.

"I'm sorry," Daniel said. It was a comprehensive apology. Father Daniel was sorry for the Gomez family, who had to separate their faith from their actions in order to survive; for Maya, who had to surrender her childhood at the altar of poverty; for the way the U.S. military polluted the island and its waters with mercury, nitrate, dieldrin, and lead that contaminated the fish and pearl oysters; and for the way the soldiers swallowed up and regurgitated the island's women and girls.

"Her photo," Mrs. Gomez said, handing Daniel an envelope. "In case you need to show somebody."

Daniel promised them that he would go to Riyalh to look for Maya.

"Let's go to the grotto and say the Nine Hour Novena," Mrs. Gomez told her husband as she stood up. "At the end of nine hours, Francis Xavier will send her back."

Daniel had trained himself not to blink at the islanders' vivacious brand of faith. Two decades on the island had taught him that in Chomumbhar, the supernatural was every bit as real as life. A dozen times in the previous year alone, one or another of his parishioners had reported witnessing the extraordinary: a statue of the Blessed Virgin that wept; an image of Jesus in the Eucharistic wafer; and inner locutions, dreams and visitations from the Holy Family and Saint Francis.

Daniel loved the island and its people. Their faith, it seemed to him, was as strong as it had been in the time of the early church. Isolated as he was from the world, following as he was in the footsteps of the first Jesuits, Daniel found himself drawn to Saint Francis Xavier. It seemed to him that they both faced similar problems. Francis Xavier had found an East peopled with natives who worshipped separate but equal gods in temples and mosques, and Portuguese infidels bent on debauchery. Daniel had found polytheists who covered all the bases by praying to all the gods, fervent Catholics, and empire builders who believed they were God.

Daniel went to Riyalh that night. For the first time in nearly ten years, he wore the brown linen robes of his order—a cowl neck tunic with a braided white cincture. He looped his rosary of large wooden beads through the cincture so it dangled from his right hip. On his feet, he wore the regulation open-toed sandals of the Jesuit. The dark attire made his pale skin, sandy hair, and blonde eyelashes appear even more striking. Daniel walked through the main square of Riyalh from end to end, Maya's photograph rolled up in the deep pocket hidden in the folds of the robe. Loud rock music blared from the street's bars and strip joints. Garish neon signs flashed the names of the clubs— *Pink Lady, Wet Candy, Lick Stick, Hot Well.* Women, mostly Eurasian, stood outside the clubs wearing G-strings, push-up bras, and spike heels. Three teenagers—a tawny triptych— giggled like teenagers everywhere, and jiggled their breasts at a group of servicemen walking by. A large banner with the words, "USS Liberty Officers and Crew, Welcome Home," hung above the entrance to the *Pink Lady*. Several bouncers stood outside the clubs. A Chinese moneychanger sat in a kiosk smoking a cheroot. Outside the *Hot Well*, a hostess sat on a bench, waiting for customers. She was wearing a lacy red bra with matching panties and red stiletto heels. Glossy red toenails, as long as her long red fingernails, peeked out from open-toed shoes. Soldiers walked by wearing fatigues and caps. Daniel was always taken aback by how young they were: more years in front of them than behind them, yet so reconciled to dying.

"I bet you know Maya Gomez," Daniel said, extending Maya's photo to her.

The woman shrugged and stared at the rosary at Daniel's waist, then looked down at her shoes.

"Her family is desperate." Daniel said, staring at her.

The woman tucked her feet under the bench, as if remembering modesty.

"They are very poor."

"She was here until last week, Father," she finally said. "You can ask inside." "Let Father in," she yelled at the bouncer standing behind her.

A domed stage, a carousel without horses, bloomed from the center of a large circular bar of polished mahogany. Servicemen sat around the bar, alone or in groups, drinking and watching the stage. Other soldiers sat in booths ringing the perimeter of the room, many with hostesses for company. On stage, a woman wearing a sequined white gown with slits cut to the thighs sang a Portuguese ballad. She caressed the poles of the carousel as she danced, moving from one to the other, pressing herself to the poles, sliding up and down. When the music stopped, the audience clapped, whistled, and howled. She descended the stairs, and walked towards an empty booth cordoned off with red ropes.

"Mariel Vega, one night with you," a young soldier hollered at her retreating back as he clasped his hands to his heart.

Daniel spotted the proprietor of the bar immediately: middle-aged, beehive hairdo, an executive manner. She stood inside the well of the bar drawing beers from a trinity of taps. Daniel introduced himself to the woman.

"Are you going to order?" Deus Mae asked.

Daniel slid the photograph across the bar.

"Not my business."

"Maya Gomez is a minor, very much your business," he said.

"She told me she was eighteen," Deus Mae said, as she filled a glass with dark stout and placed the drink in front of Daniel. "All procedures were followed with Maya. I released her to the GI only after he paid her bar fine."

Bar fine was the penalty a soldier paid to the bar owner for appropriating a girl for himself.

She retrieved a petty cash box from under the bar. She opened the box and produced a folded chit: *'Bar Fine, 1,000 Flores. Maya Gomez, Cherry Girl. Released to Corporal John Wilkes, U.S. Army.'*

"Such prices," Daniel said.

"Still not enough for loss of virgin," Deus Mae explained efficiently.

"Do you know where he might have taken her?" Daniel asked.

"As you can see, all procedures were followed with Maya." Deus Mae closed her face the way she might close her shop—down with the window shades, on with the locks, off with the lights.

Daniel called the base chaplain the next morning.

"John Wilkes? You've gotta be kidding." The chaplain promised to look into the situation.

Daniel returned to Riyalh to continue his search. The red-light district was a shadow of itself in the light of day. All the bars and most of the restaurants were closed; the moneychanger's booth was vacant. Only a few people were outside. Daniel extended Maya's photo to some soldiers. "You're pushing it, Father," a stern faced Marine told Daniel without breaking his stride.

By noon, a combination of heat, hunger, and rejection left Daniel feeling lethargic and hopeless. He settled at a table inside Koo's Noodle Shop and placed Maya's picture on the table. "*Kway Teow, chow fun*, and *ice kachang* in a tall glass," he told the stir-fry man who was cleaning his wok.

"Trail is cold by now," a woman's voice ventured.

Daniel looked up. Mariel Vega was seated at a far corner table under the shop's awnings. She was the only other customer in the place.

"She's damaged goods already, hiding somewhere in shame." Mariel twisted a forkful of cellophane noodles against a porcelain spoon.

"Her family will take her back in any condition," said Daniel.

"Of course they will. She's the paycheck," Mariel replied.

"They're good people; they love her," he said.

"Love, greed, sin. All twisted up in one big psycho mess."

Daniel stared at Mariel Vega.

"It's rude to be so bold-faced on the island, you should know." She stared back at him.

Embarrassed, Daniel turned round to watch his food being cooked. When he turned back, she had put on sunglasses.

"How long have you been doing this?" he asked, and quickly regretted it.

"How long you been a priest?"

"Too long," he said.

"When heart's in it, everything seems twice as long."

"Yeah," he agreed in that American way, long and slow in three beats.

"You hear my confession, maybe I'll help you find her," Mariel said as she pushed her sunglasses up to her crown. She picked up her bowl and carried it to Daniel's table. Mariel wore an embroidered white tunic with matching palazzo pants. Her skin was too dark to be European, too light to be Asian. Her eyes were almond-shaped and green; the straight hair that reached down to her waist was auburn.

The stir-fry man delivered Daniel's order.

"Long list of secrets. Take you through *ice kachang*," she said.

"You don't get off that easy. Come to church," Daniel said as he picked up a pair of chopsticks.

"I thought God is everywhere. Not locked up inside gold box," Mariel said.

"Sins don't sit well on an empty stomach." Daniel picked up a medallion of pork with the chopsticks.

"I didn't say I sinned." Mariel speared a fishball.

"Tell me in the confessional," Daniel said.

The click-click of their chopsticks pierced the air as they ate in silence.

After settling with the stir-fry man, Daniel and Mariel walked the main square of Riyalh. The place was stirring slowly to life. Security guards, bar owners, moneychangers, hostesses, whores, and servicemen began to appear on the sidewalks.

"Give me her photo," Mariel said as she laid her hand on his arm.

Daniel handed Maya's photo to Mariel, and sat down on a bench in front of the *Pink Lady*.

Mariel spoke in English to the Americans, Cantonese to the bar owners, Portuguese to the bargirls, and Malay to the guards. She thrust Maya's photograph under their noses.

"You tell me where she is, okay, Joe?" "She's my sister. You have heart, okay, Sam?" "Our Mama is dying; want to see Maya one last time, okay, Joe?"

"Sure, I'll tell you where she is. Tonight, my place. Don't wear nothing," a private told her. His friends cackled.

"Big dumb jerk." Mariel gave him the finger.

"Hey, Joe, you have sister and mother?" Mariel asked a sergeant as she showed him Maya's photo.

At five o'clock, when the red dirt had failed to yield up Maya, Mariel turned to Daniel. "I have to go," she said.

"Leave all this. Come to church. Make a retreat." Daniel hailed a cab.

"I have to go to work," Mariel said, as she handed Maya's photo back to Daniel.

Mariel Vega appeared at the Cathedral of the Holy Comforter during the fifth week of mangosteen season. Daniel led her through the side gate of the church down the paved walkway and the Lourdes grotto to a detached, flat-roofed shed next to the rectory.

"This is where parishioners make their retreat," Daniel said as he opened the door.

A twin bed without a headboard stood flush against one brick wall. A crucifix hung above the bed where the headboard should have been. A table with a lamp and a chair beside it stood against the adjacent wall. Above the table, a wooden shelf held a statue of a teenage Madonna in white robes with blue trim. An alcove behind the bed held a stove, sink, and laminate countertops. A bathroom was in the back of the room. A door opened out to a patch of uncut grass and the Indian Ocean in the distance.

"There are tunics hanging in the closet," said Daniel "Fruit and bread in the fridge."

"How long people stay? Maybe, I take some time off. You get answers in two weeks?" Mariel asked.

"Are you looking for answers?"

"I'm looking for nothing," she said.

"Stay or leave. Leave or stay." He left without closing the door. He thought of Francis Xavier's letter from Maurica that he had read that morning : *I have considered in what great necessity they are, with no one to instruct them or give them the sacraments, and I have come to think that I ought to provide for their salvation even at the risk of my life.*

Mariel shut the door, and fell back onto the bed. "It's all your fault," she said to the woman on the ledge, shutting her eyes.

She woke to the sound of ocean waves and glanced at the statue. Mariel had given up on God a long time ago, as soon as she found out she had to make her own way in the world. When she began to lie down with men at the *Hot Well*, she imagined the Blessed Virgin watching her soil herself. But it made her crazy. "Where I'm going, I cannot need you," she would say to herself to silence her shame. As she roused herself from sleep, she remembered what she had done. Tuesday was the short Colonel's day. A mechanical man who ran like clockwork. He would be very angry with her. The shorter the American man, the angrier he got, she had discovered. Something to do with being less instead of more, stingy in the land of plenty, a bonsai in the land of redwoods, an anomaly.

"You will never be late! Do you understand?" he might scream at her.

Once, he pulled a gun from a blazer pocket, and waved it close to her face when she had not moaned loud enough.

"For five thousand *flores*, I want you begging me to fuck you." He traced the gun across her cheek.

Panicked, Mariel screamed for Deus Mae.

"Hey!" He held her tightly by the jaw and forced her mouth towards his. "There's no crying in baseball."

Mariel tried to turn her mind to a future for herself, but she couldn't. Her past, the short Colonel, the life she lived at the *Hot Well* weighed down on her like a rock. Mariel spent the first week of her retreat in a languorous, timeless trance, getting out of bed only to eat and to relieve herself.

At the end of the second week, Daniel slipped a note under Mariel's door. "Newsbox is making tea in the kitchen," the note read. Mariel slipped on the blouse and pants she arrived in, and went to the rectory kitchen. A sparrow of a woman motioned for her to sit down.

"Father says you're from Riyalh," Newsbox poured tea already laced with milk into a glass for Mariel.

"From around there, nearby." Mariel sat down at a table and sipped the tea. The retreat had not been kind to her. She was too thin; her skin had crackled from lack of whorehouse essentials like moisturizer and makeup. What kind of man pays for a woman who looks like dying orchids? Newsbox wondered.

"You want mangosteen?" Newsbox nodded towards a comb of purple balls sitting on the counter. Mariel walked to the crop. She swirled her forefinger over the length of the comb, and chose a perfect fruit – shiny, unblemished, the color of a waxed brinjal. She returned to the table with the fruit cupped in her hands. She laced her fingers around the fruit to exert pressure in order to split it. When the shell broke in two equal pieces, Mariel placed the two halves face up on the table. She picked and devoured the white segments, two and three at a time.

Newsbox looked on with disgust. She had come by her name because she was known to spread news more effectively than CNN. She was a big mouth, everyone knew. Her husband said her tongue was so long it could be used to signal small aircraft.

"You owe me a confession." Father Daniel came into the room. He was wearing a gaudy, orange batik shirt, shorts, and floppy sandals.

"Not in those clothes," she laughed.

"As long as I have this," Daniel said, holding up a purple sash with tassels at each end.

Mariel followed the priest in his disrespectful shorts past the rectory and retreat, down the grassy path, and to the beach. "You're crazy," she said.

"You said so yourself, God is everywhere." He motioned for her to sit down.

Both of them slid to the sand. He sat cross-legged. She adjusted herself to a half kneeling position with her legs tucked under her. He placed the narrow stole around his neck, made a sign of the cross, and began the rites of the sacrament of reconciliation *silentario*.

Mariel watched his lips move, and began to sift sand through her fingers. She cupped sand in her palms and poured it from one hand to the other.

When Daniel finished the prayer, he studied her hands for a moment. Mariel dropped the sand and clutched her fists tightly.

"What do you want God to know?" Daniel said.

Mariel's head felt heavy. She wished she hadn't left the *Hot Well*. "Nothing," she said.

"You didn't leave Riyalh for nothing. What do you want to tell God?" Daniel asked.

"I don't know," Mariel said. His direct manner and steady gaze were very rude, she decided. He was trying to pin her down, make her account for her actions; she resented it.

"This is your soul's business. You need to take care of it," Daniel said, as he stood up and walked to the water's edge.

Mariel stood up, arms crossed, clutching her body. She walked into the water up to her ankles, and watched the fishing boats in the distance. A group of schoolchildren strolled past them towards the fishing village where they lived. She turned to face Daniel. "I started out as a good person," Mariel finally said.

"Some girls work in Riyalh for glamour. To dress sexy, and sit on barstools smoking cigarettes, waiting for white men to go crazy for them. I did it to feed myself, to take care of my parents."

"Deus Mae at *Hot Well* saw me at Resurrection Beach. I was fourteen. My parents were so poor they could not afford to buy me bras. Deus Mae saw that right away. She told me, 'You are beautiful; you do not have to do volume business like other girls. I will treat you like reserved stock, like the *VSOP* I lock up in glass cabinet behind the bar.' So we made a deal. She would keep me as cherry girl until I was sixteen. I would dance and sing. Nobody would touch me." Mariel bent down to wipe sea foam off her legs.

Because Mariel was small in the way many Asian women are small, and because Daniel was tall in the way many American men aim to be tall, he found himself looking at the crooked river of beige scalp where her hair parted.

"The day I turned sixteen, Deus Mae told me I would have new duties. 'You are reserved stock, therefore you will be very expensive. You will only go with officers and colonels with good manners and clean test results.' They are not like the boys trained for killing, who can only pay fifty *flores*. The other girls talk about how angry and jumpy the boys are, how they arrange themselves into fighter stance if you surprise them with a touch or a hug. When they lie down, they have killing and death still on their mind. A lot of them ask, 'Will you kill for me?' 'Will you die for me?' in the middle of their business. When they finish they say, 'I'm dying!' or 'I'm dead!'

My soldiers are gentlemen. They call me querida—darling. I am outro esposa—their other wife. They show me pictures of their families. They are all married to same kind of woman they talk about with misty eyes. Same blue-eyed children. 'We've known each other since first grade,' they say about the wife. 'She's my princess, he's going to be linebacker,' they boast about the children. Then they climb on top of me and do their business. Always with their eyes open."

Daniel rubbed his fingers in small circles over his temples to pacify a slowly mounting headache.

"Do I make you sick?" she asked.

"Say three Our Fathers, Hail Marys, and Glory Bes," he said.

She closed her eyes, clasped her hands in prayer, and recited her penance silently.

Daniel squatted down, scooped some water into his hands, and splashed it into his face. Cold woke him up; cold always did.

"You have choices, you know," he said as he rose to his feet.

"Sshh," she silenced him, her eyes still closed, still praying. She mouthed the word, amen, made a sign of the cross, and opened her eyes. "Wear goggle and mask to screw mouthpiece on telephone, fifty cents a unit. Work like donkey for Li Li Loong. What choices?" she asked.

"Don't you see the difference between right and wrong?" Daniel asked.

"When you have no choices, wrong is always right," she said.

There were so many people at High Mass that Sunday that the balcony pews usually reserved for Christmas and Easter had to be opened to accommodate the excess flow. People had come to see the woman who, Newsbox said, was a devil sent to test their faith, a woman who had taken everything between her legs. During Holy Communion, all the adults participated in the Eucharist so that they could walk past Mariel, sitting alone in the front row. They considered her proud demeanor, her head held high as if she were somebody, her lack of remorse, and most of all, her provocative act of simply being there, breathing, in their midst. And they considered Father Daniel, a handsome man who might have made someone a tender husband and lover, looking so priestly as he said Mass. Everyone concluded that the possibility of sin and fornication was definitely in the air.

In the vestry after Mass, Mariel squinted at the drops of crimson on Daniel's white chasuble.

"Mrs. Rosario bit my finger when I gave her the host." Daniel pressed the ridge below the nail of his injured thumb.

"Poor father!" Mariel hurried to the cabinet over the sink, stood on tiptoes, and rummaged through it.

"Hungry Christian," Daniel quipped.

"Maybe angry one." Mariel retrieved a box of Band-Aids. She knew she had to be careful with him. She held one up as she took his hand. He pulled back.

"Very hard for me, but I control myself with you, Father," she teased.

Daniel blushed. Twenty years a priest and he was still a bumbling idiot with women, always misreading their intentions.

It was true that Mariel had turned his head. It was true that in the course of a day, he found himself thinking about her nearly all the time, wondering what it would be like to let himself go with her. He could imagine it: holding her, tilting her head to touch her lips with the pads of his fingers before he kissed her, before he crushed her small frame to himself. Sometimes, he went further. He imagined holding her breasts, taking them in his mouth, and mounting her, penetrating the O of her. His imaginings of her felt so real, they passed for happiness. But Daniel knew that for him, wrong could never look like right.

Instead of meditating on the spiritual exercises of Ignatius Loyola like all good Jesuits, Daniel turned to Francis Xavier's journals: *Truly I have put all my trust in God, and I wish as much as is in me to obey the precept of our Lord Jesus Christ. But, when the hour comes when you see plainly that to obey God you must sacrifice life, it comes to pass that what before seemed a very clear precept is involved in incredible darkness.*

"Father, you hear about the fantastic miracle?" Mariel's long hair cloaked her face as she tended to Daniel's finger. "Mother Mary appears on the cliffs at Umayatt." She wrapped the Band-

Aid round his finger. "Instant cures, rosaries turn to gold. What do you think?" Mariel looked up at Daniel.

"I think she's a show off." Daniel pulled his hand away.

"She makes the sun dance for one hour," Mariel said.

"Ah yes, the old dance of the sun trick."

"You don't believe?" she asked.

"I think it's undignified for the Madonna to be carrying on like the Peking Circus." Daniel took the embroidered white surplice off his shoulders.

"Many people see her, not just one person," Mariel said, as she folded it and placed it in a glass-paneled armoire.

"Believing without seeing is the locus of our faith." He shed the chasuble and handed it to her; he was wearing his alb, a white linen gown.

"Poor people have to see to keep believing." She folded the chasuble so that the gold cross was centered, and placed it in the glass case. "I'm going to see her, you watch," she said.

"You're going to Umayatt?"

"With no capital except the dirt on my neck?" Mariel asked tartly.

"Well, I can't fund your excursion," Daniel said.

"I don't need money, Father. She's coming here." Mariel was sure of it.

God didn't impregnate a virgin; Jonah wasn't really in the belly of a whale; Jesus didn't visit his disciples on a beach and eat fish with them after he died; and the Blessed Virgin wasn't a circus performer. These were the Biblical fairy tales Daniel had to disbelieve, in order to maintain his faith. The way he saw it, Mariel had abandoned her brains to surrender to an easy scheme.

"I must see the Blessed Mother," Mariel insisted for the second time that day, as he went through the routine motions of shedding his vestments after sunset Mass.

Repentant sinners always wanted glamour from their religion, Daniel thought. They wouldn't settle for the workmanlike, mundane, fruitless, non-reciprocal groping in the dark of ordinary people. Half a life as a priest had taught him that he was just as ordinary and blind as everyone else. Between conducting sunrise and sunset masses fourteen times a week, giving communion and hearing confession, presiding over baptisms and last rites, officiating at weddings and funerals, counseling newlyweds and bitter spouses, leading prayer groups and visiting the homebound, the glamour had been beaten out of his faith bit by bit. And when he did slouch at the upholstered kneeler in his room at the end of each day to look for the holy, he met nothing but the inside of nothing.

"I deserve to see her," Mariel said a week later, as she folded Daniel's red chasuble, kissed the cross on his stole, and returned them to their proper place in the glass cabinet.

If anyone deserved to see the Blessed Virgin, it was he, Daniel knew. He had adopted the Madonna as his mother and cultivated a devotion to her after his own mother died of cancer when he was fifteen. Numb with grief, he had prayed. "Mary in front of me, Mary above me, Mary beside me, Mary in me," he said into the mirror each morning before he brushed his teeth. In his first year at the seminary, he was certain he would be rewarded with a Marian apparition. He prepared himself with fasting, prayer, and penance. He kept all-night rosary vigils until he crumbled to the floor from exhaustion. Instead of sleeping on a bed, he curled up on the concrete floor in his room, using his Bible for a pillow. He was on a spiritual high as he waited for her, every nerve in his body exposed and surrendered to his faith, thrilling in anticipation of her coming—of hearing the rustling, swishing sound of her robes, silk against silk. But she never came, he never saw her, and his faith grew ordinary, like everyone else's.

* * *

Mariel was still at the Cathedral and in retreat, three weeks later, during the last week of mangosteen season. Daniel wanted her gone. It was too hard for him to have her so close and so out of his reach. He could do nothing with his feelings but burn them off with prayer—"Mary in front of me, Mary above me, Mary beside me, Mary in me."

After sunset mass that Saturday, parishioners milled about the church foyer wanting Daniel's attention. Daniel dispensed advice, congratulations, and commiseration. He observed proper local form—he looked at the men when he was talking to them, and he looked at the men when he was talking to their wives. His parishioners considered him a true islander, a true pearl. However, they still worried about the undone between him and Mariel. When will she finish her retreat? they asked.

"She's leaving any day now," Daniel assured them.

Soon the foyer emptied, and Daniel found himself alone. When he looked back at the chancel, he saw Mariel clearing the low altar.

As he turned back to close the large wooden doors under the pediment, he heard the rustling, swishing sound of silk against silk. Maya's shiny, purple cheongsam looked lurid in that place. Her eyes were swollen shut from tears, scratches, and dried blood. A gash above her lip swelled outwards. Her top front teeth were missing, the two on the bottom leaned against her lower lip, ready to break from their bloody gums. The skin on her arms was stained with blue welts and burns.

"Father," she said.

"Call Mr. Gomez," Daniel told Mariel. He led Maya to a pew, kicked the cushioned kneeler up, and offered her a seat.

"Why did you go with him, Maya?" Daniel watched the blood pool around the girl's loose teeth.

"I wanted to be his wife—il real esposa, to go back with him to Kentucky."

"They're on the way." Mariel's high heels clicked loudly on the cool tiles.

"When he was at the bar, he looked so quiet and kind. He

didn't talk or shout like the others. A quiet American." Tears ran down Maya's deformed face.

"The worst kind," Daniel said, as he dabbed a cloth gently against her cheeks.

"His anger come out when we were alone. After he beat me, he felt better." Maya winced from the salt of tears and the unhinging of teeth from their posts.

"It's over now," Daniel said, holding the girl's hands in a firm grip. He pressed her hands in his so that she would believe him.

"He didn't use condom," Maya said.

Mr. Gomez arrived with Mrs. Gomez and Maya's two brothers and three sisters. When they walked into the church they looked like a sloping mountain—arranged from tallest to smallest.

"My daughter," Mr. Gomez said with a kindness that touched Maya and filled her with shame.

"Stupid!" Mrs. Gomez shouted at her daughter. "I told you to make your blood cold."

"We keep making the same mistake. From the beginning, we just kept doing everything wrong," Mr. Gomez said.

The children looked at their sister for clues.

"Give her your understanding." Daniel placed his hand on Mr. Gomez's shoulder.

Mr. Gomez looked at Maya, who was still seated on the bench. "It doesn't matter. It wasn't our fault," he finally said.

"How about Amerasian grandchild?" Mariel asked.

Mrs. Gomez rocked back on her heels as if Mariel had hit her, "You spoiled everything! Stupid, so stupid," she screamed at Maya.

"It will be all right," Daniel said gently.

"Bless you. Thank you, Father," Mr. Gomez said. He guided his family of seven to the door: five clueless children; a wife burning in anger; and a daughter seasoned in shame.

You're welcome, not at all, no problem, it was our pleasure,

97

the least we could do, Daniel thought as he closed the doors behind the family. He walked under the vaulted side aisles and stopped at one of three doors grouped together. Without switching the lights on, he entered one of the confessionals and sat on a high-backed chair. He breathed loudly, pulling air sharply to the bottom of his lungs. What he wanted to do was raise a clenched fist at the nothing but the inside of nothing.

"Give me something back," he said aloud.

"Praying in the dark is useless, you should know," Mariel's voice rose from the penitent's side of the confessional.

Daniel only knew he would close his eyes for her.

Sudden Departure

On the morning of his fifth birthday, Aslan Fahr spent several hours crying. His weeping was so violent that his nose ran, his lower eyelids swelled into red quarter moons, and his head ached. His tears had started soon after breakfast.

"Present! I want my present," he had badgered his mother, wailing like a muezzin calling the faithful to morning prayer. He tugged at her sarong and clutched the rolls of fat on her arms as he begged for his present.

"Get off me! Get out of my sight!" Narimah Fahr had snapped, as she sat at the kitchen table cleaning a mound of prawns. She was pulling the shell casings off the prawns and ripping off their heads. She flailed her arms to push Aslan away as if she was swatting a mosquito. At one point, she elbowed him in his ribs, not hard enough to hurt him, but just rough enough to warn him.

Nevertheless, he kept it up, an unrelenting, unremitting litany. "I want my toy." "Where is my toy?"

Narimah Fahr sat with her prawns, her face frozen in a state of calm as she ignored the child. She sliced the curled backs of the giant shrimps, ripped the strings of feces from their sides, and plunged the prawn butterflies in a bowl of cold water.

Aslan leaned his whole body into her. His nose tickled from the gardenia scent on her nape.

After half an hour, she stood up with the prawns in one hand and a bag of entrails in another, and walked towards the double sink. She rinsed the meat in a colander and tapped the enamel against the side of the sink.

When Aslan tugged at her sarong again, she set the colander at the edge of the sink and turned to look down at him. She stood with her back to the sink, her large rump practically falling inside it, and wiped her hands on a tea towel.

Narimah Fahr had a large, round, fat head, and small, flat features that occupied too little of her face, so that in profile she seemed to be without lips or eyes. Her hair was braided and coiled into a bun.

"Are you ready for your present?" she asked, narrowing her eyes as she looked at a spot above his head.

Aslan breathed in deeply to control his tears, his runny nose, his crying, and nodded vigorously. She told him to sit down and wait. She left the room, and came back with a package bound in newspaper.

It looked to Aslan as if it had been hastily wrapped, maybe even that minute.

"This is for being a good boy," she said, extending the package to him.

Aslan hurriedly ripped the paper off it.

"For a good, good boy," Aslan's mother said.

It was a woman's undergarment, a pair of his mother's large floral panties. When Aslan looked up at his mother, confused, she laughed so hard a bubble of mucus flew out of her nose.

"Wear it like this," she said, and pulled it over his head like a hat.

Aslan ran out of the kitchen tearing the panties off his head and hurling it across the room. He climbed onto the imposing wrought iron swing on the verandah of the Fahr home, and rocked himself to a fast, clipped rhythm. He clutched the suspension wires of the swing tightly as he watched the mouth of the lane. Any minute, his father would turn the curve of the lane leading to the complex of lemon-colored houses where the Fahr family lived. Aslan wanted so badly to see his father that he willed himself not to blink. He opened his eyes wide so that his long eyelashes nearly touched the top of his eyelids. He stopped swinging as soon as he saw his father.

Idris Fahr worked as a doctor's aide at a government dispensary fifteen minutes from the cul-de-sac of yellow bungalows. "Thirteen minutes if I walk briskly, eleven if the traffic lights are in my favor," Idris would say.

He was a fastidious man, forever checking the time on two wristwatches that he wore close together on his right hand. The watch closest to his knuckles announced island time; the other was set to Greenwich Mean Time—a nod to his youth when a respected medical career in England had seemed within his grasp.

"What have I got for you, do you think?" Idris asked, ambling toward the swing. He made a big show of a package hidden behind his back. It was wrapped in glossy paper and festooned with curled green and blue ribbons.

"I don't even know," Aslan said as he lurched at his father from the swing. His thin arms circled his father's hips as he twisted his head around his father to catch a peek. He pressed his cheek into his father's stomach.

"Nothing at all," Idris said. He arched his back and craned his neck to look at the package. "Just my bum."

Aslan giggled.

Father and son jostled each other playfully as they made their way to the kitchen.

Idris barely looked at his wife, who stood near the stove dipping sliced bananas in batter to make fritters, or at Sharifah, his thirteen-year-old daughter, who had come downstairs for snacks. She was seated at the kitchen table, fritters piled on a plate in front of her.

Idris smiled at Aslan as he rotated the package in front of him. He drew a chair from the kitchen table and sat down with his legs wide apart.

Aslan stood facing Idris, his hands resting on his father's knees.

"Any calls?" Idris said. He tried to untie the ribbons, first with his thick fingers, then with his teeth.

"Is this a hotel?" Mrs. Fahr flashed an angry look at her husband.

Aslan clutched the material of his father's trousers, and looked up at him.

"No. It is not a hotel," Idris murmured. He stroked the boy's hair to comfort him.

"The hotel is closed," Mrs. Fahr said. She waved a ladle in the air for effect.

Narimah Fahr would have loved to start a good fight, a screaming epic dragged out over days. She would accuse him of treating her like a slave, of ignoring her, of wanting a mistress, of trying to kill her. "You're not a man," she would say, or, "There's nothing between your legs." She would hold nothing back except the thing she really wanted to say, and could not bring herself to admit—that she hated the boy for being the center of Idris's very life, the planet around which he orbited.

Idris never offered a rebuttal. It was true. They were one, Idris and Aslan, giving light and life only to each other while his wife and daughter stood in the shadows, embalmed in fat and fury.

Before Aslan was born, Idris avoided going home during the Empty Hour. Even twenty minutes in the company of his wife and daughter, as they sipped cardamom tea and scoffed sweetmeats by the pound, reduced him to melancholy. It seemed to him, his life was divided into two pathetic halves: the lowly job at the dispensary, daily proof of his failure; and his family, two women he rejected on principle. After all, Narimah Lal had interfered with his plans to go to medical school in England by getting herself pregnant. He never forgave her for her untimely mistake. Idris's dark mood would remain with him until he returned to the dispensary.

It was Narimah who decided that giving Idris a son would force him to forgive her. She went from one holy man to another, from windward to leeward, hopping from Chomumbhar to the smaller islands, in search of mystics and monks who would give her a miracle. She visited holy men who prayed over her and gave her amulets to wear, stones to keep in her pockets, potions to drink, and instructions on how and when to copulate. One holy man told her that the correct position for conceiving a boy was for the woman to be on top during relations. Another told her that sexual organs should point to the East where everything begins. Narimah moved the bed, which had previously been pointing in a northerly direction. That night, in her re-aligned bed, she reached for her husband. "I want to put things right between us," she said, straddling him, riding him, grinding into his waist. To her satisfaction, she was pregnant before the next monsoon. Idris Fahr had rejoiced when the sonographer at the ultrasound clinic pointed out the penis of the fetus.

Aslan watched patiently as his father broke the colorful ribbons, and pressed the torn paper under his shoes. When the task was complete, Aslan stepped on the paper, which crunched noisily under his feet. Idris held the boy in the arc of his legs, and together they balanced the object in front of them. Idris curved his arms around Aslan's, covering Aslan's tiny limbs with his own.

"Guess what it is, Assie?"

"I don't know!" The boy jumped up and down, his small wiry body jerking from a tremor of excitement and frustration.

"It's how Imran Khan got to play cricket at Lord's," Idris said.

Mrs. Fahr snorted.

"You shut up," Idris shot back, as he admired the cricket bat.

"What's Imran Khan?" Aslan asked, stroking the heavy wood.

Sharifah looked up from her homework. "Wasn't he the best batsman ever?" she asked.

"Absolutely. He had the world at his feet," Idris said.

Sharifah smiled. Then, remembering that her mother would not approve of her smiling at her father, she looked down at her books.

"He'll break his head open with it," Mrs. Fahr said, looking up from her fritters, her fingers soaked in batter.

"Malacca willow. The finest," Idris explained to the boy. "It won't make a plunk like balsa."

"Why didn't you get him a plastic one?" Mrs. Fahr tried to soothe an itch on her cheek with the slope of her shoulder.

"Do you think Yehudi Menuhin's father gave him a plastic violin?" Idris asked.

Narimah Fahr did not reply, as she did not know who Yehudi Menuhin was. There was so much in her marriage that remained unknown to her: why she had married Idris Fahr, why she couldn't make him happy despite having given him a son, why she was angry with him. Yet there would have been no marriage at all if she had not pursued him, the doctor to be, and impressed him with the taste of her cooking, and the volume of her orgasms. It seemed to her that Idris and she were forever separated, stranded on two sides of a Ganges, one of them in possession of a boat, the other an oar, and neither of them willing to save the other. She considered Idris a failure, and considered herself one too, for not divining his mediocrity in the first place.

Narimah Fahr had grown fat from clarified butter and unshed tears. Where other women of her curdled temperament volunteered at temples and schools, using heightened activity, like tiger balm or nutmeg oil, to soothe away the pains of an arthritic marriage, she spent many hours in the kitchen making traditional sweetmeats and cakes. Her culinary output impressed no one; its only function seemingly to triple the girth of her daughter, and double her own bulk.

"This is the real thing. A holy thing," Idris Fahr's eyes shone with love as he looked at his son.

"Look at it! Bigger than he is. He can hardly carry it," Mrs. Fahr said.

"We're going to the exhibition match in July." Idris Fahr got up from the chair as if to settle the matter. He held his son and the bat aloft as he rose. "Australia-Sri Lanka, it will be a slaughter," he said as he kissed the boy on his cheek.

"What is that to us?" Narimah grumbled as she turned over the fritters in the pan.

The day after Aslan's birthday, Idris Fahr sent a telegram to Mark's & Spencer's in London's Oxford Street. He enquired about "the best first-class cricket suit for a five–year-old that money could buy." A week later, Idris received a letter from the store's manager, John Quigley, Esq. He informed Idris Fahr that they did not carry cricket suits for five-year-olds, but that cricket attire of the finest cotton, and summer-weight wool spun in the upper Hebrides, could easily be custom made. He recommended Carlton Taylor's, Clothiers for Men, on Bond Street. Mr. Quigley offered to supervise the order for a small fee. He asked Idris Fahr to send Aslan's measurements.

Idris Fahr hurried home from the dispensary carrying the blue Par Avion envelope from London and a green measuring tape. He placed the tape between Aslan's legs to measure his inseam, his waist, his hips, his length, and his rise. When Idris placed the tape under Aslan's armpits to measure his chest, Aslan laughed uncontrollably from the tape as well as his father's tickles.

Six weeks later, Idris Fahr took Aslan, dressed in the best first-class cricket attire that money could buy, to the Australia-Sri Lanka match at the Suri Club in Port Contadu.

Everyone responded to the boy's dashing appearance. A dowager wearing all her wealth on her arms, gold and diamond-studded bangles from wrist to elbow, sighed when she saw Aslan. "So, so sweet." She shook her head and smiled at the boy.

"We'll see your boy at Lord's yet, eh?" Dr. Said, Idris Fahr's supervisor at the dispensary tipped his hat.

"He will be my masterpiece," his father, the artist, beamed.

As Aslan grew up, people on the island grew accustomed to seeing him in white clothing. White spun-cotton shirt, sleeves rolled up three inches above the wrist, white cashmere vest with blue piping, white fine twill pants, white cap, white leather shoes, and his bat. Each year, Aslan's father took his measurements and sent them in a telegram to Carlton Clothiers of Bond Street. Knight in need of new armor stop bank certified cheque to follow stop.

Aslan turned heads, looking so full of promise, as he walked through the streets of Chomumbhar in his cricket regalia, glowing from the sun, swinging his bat for his father, carrying in his energetic gait his love for the game. Even at school, Aslan wore his cricket uniform through all the tortures of math, science, physics, and geography.

His father encouraged him. "Don't end up like me," Idris told his son. "I sold myself to the lowest bidder." Aslan would go to England, his father told him. He would enroll in technical school near St. John's Wood, within sight of Lord's. He would start out playing cricket in the county league. It was Idris's dream for Aslan to be an international batsman like Imran Khan, to have a test match debut at Lord's like Imran Khan.

"To play cricket is to be brave, to be resolute in the face of danger," Idris would tell the teenager. He told Aslan the story of the Ashes, matches between Australia and England that vied for the ashes of a ball used in a game long ago. He told him about Imran Khan, international batsman for Pakistan who graduated Oxford with Honors, and took the cricket world by storm. "I had the honor of seeing him play," he told Aslan.

Idris watched as his son's body memorized and learned and translated the language of cricket: fast bowls and short pitches; spinning and hard hitting; square legs and late glides; and capturing wickets. He looked on with satisfaction as Aslan began to understand the complexity of the game and grew serious about it. He played his shots with ease but, even more importantly, Aslan understood the pitch and the wicket. When the captain and the coach of the island's junior league began to take notice of Aslan, Idris was thrilled. Idris noticed that when it rained and the wicket was slick, the captain sent out the dimwits, the pace bowlers, to dry out the wicket before fielding Aslan.

Idris was very proud when the league chose Aslan to compete in a weekend international at the Suri Club with a touring team from England. Idris saw the opportunity as Aslan's debut, the poetic beginning of Aslan's ascent to the top of the cricket world.

Aslan was brilliant all around; he was in good form both bowling and batting. He scored seventy impressive runs against the English and hauled three wickets while only giving up sixty-three runs.

"This is just the beginning." His father hugged him after the game.

"You dominated the match, no question," Idris said, as they walked home from the Suri Club.

Aslan was happy and tired. He felt no need to talk, content to listen to his father basking in the glory of his achievement.

"You could try out for Worcester. Imran Khan didn't do too badly by them."

Aslan looked at his father in disbelief.

"I have money put away to get you all the way to Lord's." Idris held his son's face in his hands.

Aslan Fahr played four more internationals that came to the island that year. Most remarkably, Aslan averaged forty runs a game after his first five matches.

One Friday morning, Aslan, with his father's blessing, took the day off from school. He had been at the Suri Club for more than two hours, practicing batting in the nets, when his team captain pointed at Aslan's sister, Sharifah. She was standing behind the waist-high manicured hedge, her hands cupped like a megaphone. Aslan saw her lips flap, but could not make out what she was saying.

"Go see what the elephant wants," the captain said.

Aslan walked to the spot near the hedge where his sister was standing. "We're playing, can't it wait?"

"Something happened. Come home," she said.

"I'm going out in three," he said, sweeping his arm to point at his team, who were all looking impatiently at their batsman.

"You come now," commanded his sister.

Aslan offered a thumbs down gesture to his captain to retire himself from the game. "I'll come back," he yelled. He shrugged and pointed at his sister, to place the blame squarely where it belonged.

Aslan vaulted the hedge. "What do you do that for?" he screamed at Sharifah.

"Mummy won't let me tell you." She broke away from him and ran towards home.

Aslan thought for a moment of returning to the game, but decided to go home instead. Tea and some of his mother's *keseri* and *falooda* would go down very nicely, he thought as he walked home, twirling his bat.

Aslan arrived home, and saw a parade of slippers, shoes, and sandals lined up against the wall next to the front door. Relatives and neighbors from the cul-de-sac stood about the living room. A small ring of people huddled in the center of the room. Rugby players, Aslan thought, and giggled at his own joke. He heard a woman moan from somewhere inside the circle. A cold, clammy, irrational fear unfurled immediately in

Aslan's gut. It spread through him from the pit of his stomach up to his throat, like a snake unrolling its length. "What's going on?" Aslan looked around the room.

Aslan's mother emerged from the circle. She was dry-eyed, he noted.

"A sudden departure," Aslan's mother said, looking not at him but at the blue piping on the collar of his vest. "Just like that, your father went."

"Went where?" he asked, impatiently.

"He's dead," Mrs. Fahr said.

That was a bloody lie. He wanted to strike her.

"Tell him. Tell him everything," Mrs. Fahr turned to a man as young, as alive, and as animated as Aslan's father had been when Aslan had last seen him that morning.

"Killed by a speeding car on his way to work," the man said. He put his arm around Aslan. "God has his own reason."

Idris Fahr had gone for a walk and wouldn't be coming back: nothing glamorous or meaningful that would help Aslan make sense of it.

The day passed slowly. Aslan felt as if he were asleep, but with his eyes wide open. He sat on the swing outside the house, rocking it whenever he felt bereft. He stared at the mouth of the lane. Aslan found that if he rocked the swing hard enough until it rattled at the hinges, his brain and his thoughts would bounce violently inside his skull, and much of his pain could be shocked into submission.

During the Empty Hour, a black truck reversed onto the verandah. Aslan looked on passively, rocking the swing only enough to make it creak—a long grating noise like a howling wind, *creeek wish, creeek wish.*

Three of Aslan's male relatives, his mother's people, came out of the house and held a long spirited discussion with the driver. The four men argued among themselves in a dialect not familiar to Aslan. After listening to the driver, the trio went back inside the house. Aslan continued to rock the swing.

The men drew six chairs from the dining room. They pulled the chairs away from the table, two at a time, scraping the wooden legs against the tile floor. They arranged the chairs in the center of the living room in two rows facing each other, a foot of space between the rows. The men hurried to the truck and unloaded the coffin holding Idris Fahr. The driver helped the men carry the coffin. They staggered into the living room with the box. They positioned it over the makeshift platform and lowered it to the seats. Despite their best efforts, the coffin landed with a thud.

Narimah Fahr, Sharifah, and the neighbors gathered around the coffin. The hearse driver undid the latches and opened the coffin.

Aslan remained on the swing, rocking himself harder and harder—*creeekwish, creeekwish.* Aslan would not go near the body. Through his peripheral vision, he could see his father's sharp features above the rim of the coffin. Aslan's father was buried the next day. No one cried, except Dr. Said from the dispensary.

At breakfast a few days later, Aslan was dipping toast into runny egg yolk, and remembering how his father had promised to take him to the Ashes that year. His mother fluttered into the room waving a telegram. It was from his uncle, Tariq Fahr, his father's younger brother in America. *Held up at franchise conference in Houston stop regret absence stop coming soon stop.*

Aslan's uncle arrived a week later. He no longer called himself Tariq Fahr.

"Call me Terry," he drawled in an American accent.

Terry Fahr wore a polo shirt and crumpled khaki shorts that stopped at the thigh, baggy in front and stretched tightly across his wide rump. He was dressed in the way little boys, relieved from the national obligation to modesty, were dressed on the island. The sight of him was so strange, neighbors and their children stood outside the house to see how America could change a man.

Idris Fahr's grave was still a mound of brown dirt when Terry Fahr went to pay his respects, in his khaki shorts. Hearts and circles of marigolds, chrysanthemums, and white lilies lay over the grave. An unusual chill had preserved the wreaths so that they looked as fresh as they did on the day of the funeral.

"I guess he was needed up there," Terry Fahr comforted Aslan as he pointed vaguely to somewhere in the sky.

"He died like a dog," Mrs. Fahr said. "Left us in such a mess."

Terry Fahr took his sister-in-law's hand.

"If it wasn't for you ..." Mrs. Fahr stared into Terry Fahr's eyes.

"Don't worry about a thing." He squeezed her hand.

When Aslan came downstairs for breakfast the next day, he found his mother, sister, and Terry Fahr in the kitchen. They stopped talking as soon as he came into the room. Mrs. Fahr looked pleased with herself. Aslan had never seen her looking so well. She was fully made up as if she were going out to a party. Her eyes were blackened with kohl; a cat's whisker of liner was drawn past the natural line of the eyes. Her olive complexion was glazed with peach tones from a foundation bottle. She wore bright red lipstick, brighter than the red of the island's mailboxes. Her long hair, taken out of its coil and net, fell down her back. Terry Fahr sat very close to her, his beefy shoulders grazing hers. The thought crossed Aslan's mind that his mother was sleeping with Terry Fahr. Sharifah sat across from the pair.

"What?" Aslan said.

"We've agreed Uncle will take you to America," Narimah Fahr said.

"Papa had money put away for me to get to Lord's," Aslan said.

"I am sure he meant to, but he never got round to it," his mother said.

"He told me since I was this high. He had money saved for my cricket, to live in St. John's Wood, to go to technical school, to start in the county league," Aslan said.

"He was too young to think about dying. He thought he had time," his mother said.

"He had only his pay check and five thousand *flores* in savings," his uncle added.

"That's for Sharifah's dowry," Aslan's mother said quickly.

"He told me! He told me every day!" Aslan cried.

"What is cricket? Just childish things," his mother said.

It happened so fast, how Aslan's life spun out of control after his father's death. His whole life had gone slowly until then. He had grown impatient with the pace of the island, where time itself stood still, and life traveled around it in circles, and returned people to the same place. To church, and mosque, and temple; to Friday shopping in the dark at the night markets, and Sunday shopping and dining at Change Alley; to weeklong weddings of excess, and celebrations of escape; to Suri Club and Resurrection Beach. He had worried about ever getting off the island, and then in four weeks, life as he knew it had combusted. Everything that had kept him safe was under a mound of marigolds, chrysanthemums, and white lilies.

Aslan's uncle took him to a round of appointments at the American Embassy for his visa, and to Dr. Said's dispensary for vaccinations. Terry Fahr went to Change Alley and bought Aslan a black hard-shell Samsonite. Aslan folded up his life into the suitcase: four pairs of jeans, six shirts, twelve changes of underwear, twelve pairs of socks, and his cricket whites. He put his bat into its long, thin canvas case.

A month after his father's death, Aslan was in New York with his uncle in the back of a limousine pulling out of JFK airport. His uncle initiated a lengthy conversation with the driver: "How did the Mets do? Way to go! Are you kidding me? They need their butts kicked. Go figger. Ged owdda heer! Okay, guy. Have a good one."

Even before the jet lag wore off, Aslan's uncle woke him up. It was still dark as Terry Fahr backed his gold Oldsmobile slowly out of the garage, and reached across the front passenger seat to open the door for Aslan. Terry Fahr turned on sports radio as he entered the street from the alley. "Godda see how my boys are doin'," he said, smiling at Aslan. Terry Fahr exited the Midtown tunnel, drove down Fifth Avenue, swung west, and pulled up at a neon-lit storefront on Broadway. He got out of the vehicle and swept his hands in a large majestic arc—the way Saladin might have shown someone the breadth of his empire. "Liberty Bagels, proud purveyors of the Great American Bagel since 1990," read a large sign on the plate glass.

"1990 is not so old," Aslan mumbled.

"Ten years here is as old as a hundred somewhere else." His uncle smiled proudly.

"Watch and learn," Terry Fahr told Aslan. He showed him how to open the doors, turn right for the top lock, left for the bottom. "Once you open the door, you have twenty five seconds to deactivate the burglar alarm." He showed Aslan how to operate the cash register.

Aslan was bleary-eyed as Terry Fahr explained every aspect of Liberty Bagel to him. How to make a bagel, how to refrigerate cream cheese, how to make a cappuccino and espresso, which Terry Fahr pronounced "capazino" and "expresso." Before long, two businessmen came into the store.

"I'm throwing you at the deep end." Terry Fahr put an apron round Aslan's neck. The men studied the bagels behind glass cases as if they were ruminating the Runes.

"Tawl skim lahte and a chedar sahmun," Aslan heard one of the men say. He looked blankly at the man. Aslan's ears were used to English spoken with an island accent.

"He's in training," Terry Fahr said, and helped them with their order.

All day, Aslan's uncle told him what to do, and when he looked at his uncle in a state of utter confusion, his uncle completed the action all the while explaining every move to Aslan. "For this lady, you slice and toast the jalapeno bagel, then you take the tub of salsa cream cheese, and then you …"

Aslan's heart sank; the snake in his stomach unrolled its length. From the time Aslan was five years old, he had learned to do only one thing—cricket. It was more than enough, his father had told him.

At eleven that night, Terry Fahr drove Aslan to the house in Queens. "Piece of cake. You'll manage," he said, before turning on sports radio.

After a week, Terry Fahr ceased giving directions and pointed at Aslan when customers stepped up to the cash register. After three, Terry Fahr waited for Aslan to unlock the door each morning, and told him to make him a capazino to go while he set up the cash register.

"Have a nice day. Squeeze the tits of capitalism for me. Call me at the office if anything," Terry Fahr would say as he walked out of the door, capazino in hand.

He would return at nine each night to count the day's takings. He'd put the coins and bills in an envelope and place it in his briefcase. Twenties and fifties, which were rare in the bagel shop, went into the belly wrap Terry Fahr wore around his waist. The brown alligator belt with a large pouch in the middle made him look comically pregnant. After closing the shop, Terry and Aslan would make the trek to Queens, sports radio boring a hole in Aslan's forehead.

After a month, Terry Fahr called Aslan at the store while he was toasting an everything bagel for a woman who did not care to look at him.

"I have a customer," Aslan said.

"Good boy, good boy," Terry Fahr said.

Aslan put his uncle on hold while he attended to the woman. When he picked the telephone up again, the line was dead. Aslan dialed the number of Far East Trading, his uncle's wholesale imports business.

Terry Fahr owned Far East Trading with a partner, Ari Navidad, an islander who had bankrupted every enterprise he had ever attempted in Chomumbhar. It was common knowledge on the island that Ari Navidad was a *defeito*—a defeat, an error. Ari had been married to Karin Rodriguez, only child of Rohan Rodriguez, press secretary to Prime Minister Ferdinand D'Souza. Despite his connections to one of Chomumbhar's first families, despite his father-in-law's influence to ease his way in the world, Ari had ruined every company that had accommodated him, leaving hemorrhaged bank accounts in his wake. He was a charming dilettante, an unbridled reprobate, an irrefutable failure. Islanders joked that Ari was their Princess Margaret. He drove fast cars, drank martinis by the gallon, smoked Gauloise cigarettes through a holder, and fooled around with nurses just to have access to pharmaceuticals. He had stumbled from one absurd business to another: rerouting sugar from the Philippines, pirating Hollywood blockbusters, selling air rights to Tokyo skyscrapers, organizing a Miss Edge of the World pageant with himself as the judge, until his father-in-law had secured for him the post of Tourism Minister.

The father-in-law had believed that Ari's gregarious nature, if harnessed, would be a boon to tourism on the island. He could not have predicted that Ari would turn the small island of Tio into a haven for hedonists. Australian surfers in Day-Glo spandex shorts, American backpackers with beer bellies and libidos, and morphine-addled Israeli soldiers suffering post-traumatic stress disorder began visiting Tio. It also became a magnet for pedophiles and pleasure seekers from the First World looking for steamy sex on the Equator.

Prime Minister D'Souza and Lady Lalitha were horrified by the caliber of tourist. "We will have to start issuing pariah and low class visas soon," Lady Lalitha complained. The PM and First Lady told Ari Navidad that he had opened the floodgates to Western decadence and perversion. The son-in-law was reprimanded after the Ministry of Culture arrested a group of elderly tourists for uncultured behavior and fornication on a public beach. Ari being Ari, he continued his errant ways: he dipped into the Tourism Board's budget to settle his personal debts. During an audit, Lady Lalitha learned that many million *flores* had disappeared from the accounts. She accused Ari of national plunder, called him a traitor, and campaigned for his arrest and imprisonment. It had been the talk of the island, that only his father-in-law's personal, written appeal to the Prime Minister and Lady Lalitha had spared Ari a lengthy holiday at Dalimar Prison. What a letter that must have been; his words must have had wings, people said. America allowed Ari Navidad to start again from scratch. In America, he would reinvent himself: reveal a new layer, a new self, like a snake shedding skin.

"I've been thinking about what a great job you're doing," Terry Fahr said. "But if you keep pulling in the hours like you've been doing, you'll burn out."

"Yeah, I'm whacked," Aslan admitted.

"Here's what I'm thinking," his uncle said. "If you cut out the commute, you'd save yourself two hours each way. Give you time to unwind, listen to music, relax," Terry Fahr said. "How does that sound?"

"Sounds good," Aslan replied.

"That room in the basement, next to the storage. Why don't you move in there?" Terry Fahr suggested.

Every day, at four in the morning, Aslan Fahr would wake up to the sound of a tinny alarm clock. He would dress in the dark in his Liberty Bagel t-shirt, Liberty Bagel apron, Liberty Bagel visor, and Liberty Bagel black pants. He would climb the rickety stairs and switch on the fluorescent lights in the shop. He'd brush his teeth at the sink in the men's restroom, and splash water on his face. There were no showers in the shop's restrooms, so he gave himself sponge baths at the sinks.

Aslan would then proceed to the bakery in the middle of the shop and start his day. He would make thirteen kinds of bagels: plain, egg, cheddar, onion, sesame, everything, veggie herb, jalapeno, sundried tomato, pumpkin, raisin, blueberry, apple, and Liberty, the house signature bagel. He would not eat the bagels on principle: he was an imprisoned cricket player. His father would have approved. Instead, he filled himself on the snack bags of potato chips delivered to the store by the Frito Lay man, Chiquita bananas, and tubs of Dannon yogurt in the store's freezer.

For the most part, other than the customers who streamed in and out of Liberty Bagel for breakfast and lunch, Aslan was alone. Terry Fahr appeared twice each day. In the morning, on his way to his import business, he would stop at the bagel shop. He'd set up the cash register with a fifty-dollar float. He'd unroll the dimes, quarters, nickels and pennies from their paper wrappers, count the singles and fives, and deposit them in separate drawers.

At nine at night, Tariq Fahr would come in to tally the cash register total with the cash in the drawer, change the roll of paper, and slip the money into a large brown envelope. "Money is your uncle's alpha and omega," Aslan's father had once said of Tariq Fahr.

"Thanks to you, your sister will be all right." Terry Fahr

would hand Aslan a ten-dollar bill. He would always wave at Aslan as he headed to the door. "Don't do anything I wouldn't do," he would say, as he fished his car keys out of the pocket of his stiff leather jacket. "Catch you later," he'd say, clicking his tongue and grinning, as he pointed his finger in the shape of a gun at Aslan.

One day, Aslan was rolling bagels in a tray of poppy seeds when he heard his father's voice. "Don't be like me." Mind tricks, Aslan thought. I am alone so much the bagels are talking to me.

When his uncle came to the store that night, as usual, and went through his routine, closing the cash register, Aslan looked at him with a fixed stare.

"I'm not accusing you of anything. But we're short, guy. Seven dollars, " Terry Fahr said.

"I don't know," Aslan said, fighting sleep, fighting to keep his eyes open.

"You're putting me in a difficult position. Know what I'm saying?" his uncle said.

"I don't know what happened."

Terry Fahr banged the cash register shut so hard, Aslan's tip jar broke and scattered small change on the floor. Terry grabbed Aslan by the neck and slammed him against the espresso machine.

"Here are the rules. Don't fuck with my money," Terry Fahr said.

Aslan felt his eyes glass over with tears. "My father said you read and shit at the same time because you're a miser," he spat. He wished his father were there. He shoved Terry Fahr in the ribs and ran downstairs to the basement.

Aslan locked himself in his room and threw himself on his cot. His room was directly below the counter in the bagel shop upstairs. Noises from the shop worked their way through the pipes that ran down the wall of Aslan's room. "Yeah, we have pumpernickel," he heard his uncle tell a customer. "Yeah, we could do a BLT. You want it toasted?"

Aslan sat up on the cot and slid his legs down to the floor. He bent forward and pulled out the black Samsonite, which was under the bed. He rotated the suitcase so the latches faced him, and clicked the locks open. He retrieved his cricket whites from the case, and stroked the soft material of the vest and pants—the best first-class cricket whites money could buy. He took off the visor from his head and the apron with the Liberty logo on it. Shedding his pants and Liberty Bagel t-shirt, he quickly put on his whites. Aslan looked at himself in the cheap mirror hanging on the door. It distorted and exaggerated his features. "You are not me," he said to the mirror. From the canvas holder hanging from a nail near the door, he took out his bat. He heard his uncle come down the stairs.

"Aslan. Assie, don't be like that. Come out now. Let bygones be bygones."

Aslan gripped the handle of his bat and held it away from his body.

"Papa," he mouthed the words.

Aslan Fahr does not know which American city blinks outside his window anymore. He has been to so many. He lives in a blur of Greyhound buses taking him to nowhere. As he enters a new state – Ohio, Illinois, Iowa, Nebraska, Idaho – he gazes at fields of corn that never forget how to be yellow, bales of golden hay squatting like sumo wrestlers, giant sunflowers bowing with their burdens. In nearly every town, he sees crosses that announce the Savior's death for everybody's sins. At the bus terminals, transients of every stripe hurry to claim the limited bench spaces. They mark their turf with bags and newspapers, lie down on their duffle bags, and cover themselves with their coats. Aslan watches them: young people who move around so they don't have to think, old people who forget they have earned the right to stay in one place. Aslan keeps his eyes down; he is afraid of provoking anyone. He sleeps sitting up, his luggage wedged between his legs, his long, quilted coat draped over him, his hands snug in its sleeves so no one will try to steal it while he dozes. At rest stops, he takes change from his pockets and feeds the machines, loyal things that never fail to deliver: Cheez-Its, Mars Bar, Frito-Lay, Coca-Cola. He has seven hundred and seventy dollars left in Terry Fahr's belly wrap. He holds on to his bat, Malacca willow streaked with red and ochre. Sometimes he swings it hard and fast so it slices the air with a loud whoosh, as if decapitating a ferocious threat. He waits patiently for another bus to take him and his Samsonite further, further, away, away.

The Sum of All Sins

(1980s – 2000s)

ISLAND MAIL REVIEW

Miss Edge of the World beauty pageant announced.

Relations between US and island strained. PM urges talks.

Former cricket player returns home. Mother says he's retired.

PM calls Zela "five-footer and mental midget."

Father Daniel Sullivan meeting with SOJ superiors in Rome to discuss his future.

Interfaith clergy pray at Resurrection Beach, invoke Francis Xavier, for peace in the world.

Prison Letters of Ferdinand D'Souza

David Evans,   17th Jan
Asian Affairs Correspondent – SNN.

David,

Since General Zela and his National Front staged their coup d'état against my government, you have broadcast a stream of blatant fabrications about my leadership. These lies have grown ever more egregious and despicable, that I can no longer ignore them. Zela's first public comment after taking office on January 8th, that I had resigned in disgrace, was a diabolical lie. He afforded me no such dignity. Instead, he sent his armed thugs to the Palace to arrest me as if I was a common hooligan.

I am being held in solitary confinement here in Dalimar Prison. Lady Lalitha and our son, Ferdinand Jnr., are under house arrest at our retreat on Tilika Peak. I do not know the fate of my Deputy Prime Minister, but my full Cabinet is in detention. Rohan Rodriquez, my sterling Press Secretary, who was indispensable to me, who wrote all my speeches, who gave my words wings, was alone appropriated to serve in Zela's administration. It is galling to hear Zela, who could not utter five words without tripping over them, sounding more and more like me—an international statesman. The bastard sounded positively Nehruesque talking to Paula Zahn last night.

My incarceration is a travesty, and I mean for the international community to know what has been done to me. Despite all the lies disseminated by you and others, the truth will prevail. If you are any kind of self-respecting journalist at all, you will undoubtedly want to know the events as they occurred. I invite you to correspond with me via the courier standing in front of you. He is fully paid for and in my debt, and can be trusted to the degree that I bribe him. You may also feel safe in the knowledge that he is illiterate and cannot interfere with our exchanges.

Ferdinand D'Souza

Prime Minister, Republic of Chomumbhar.

Ferdinand, my son,   18th Jan --12.47 AM

It is late, yet I cannot sleep. The 60-watt bulb in my cell remains lit around the clock, so that day and night fuse together into a seamless eternity. My mind is clouded when I wake up, and I fumble through the mustard glow disoriented, not knowing if I should be asleep or awake, not knowing if I've slept too little or too much. It is a terrible violation of a person's primal need to return to the womb at night. How can one rest? I sleep without dreams.

After surrendering my very life to the needs of our country, after endowing it with my grand vision and imbuing it with my dreams, I am now housed in a cage like a beast. A cell that I can sum up in its entirety by walking eight tight paces this way, and nine brief paces that way. Steel bars dominate one wall, so that I am in public view at all times. A cot is bolted to the opposing wall, where a barred window affords ventilation and a crippled view. A WC and a washbasin with a faulty tap are tucked behind a four-foot high cement screen flush against the right wall. I want you to know what I endure not to hurt you, but to drive you to liberate Chomumbhar from Zela and his band of thugs. They must stand trial for sedition.

Father

Lalitha, my dearest,   19th Jan

The Red Cross representative, Sister John Bosco, brought me your letter and parcels this morning. It was good of you to send my reading glasses, and of course, the photograph. The guard did not open the letter, but did search the parcel. When his eyes fell on the official photograph of the Presidential Visit, he started blinking furiously and began to break out in a sweat. He practically genuflected in front of me. Imbecile! Why did it take a photograph of you and me standing with President and Mrs. Kennedy for him to remember that I am the Prime Minister?

Before breakfast, as I was behind the wall performing my ablutions, he and the other fellow loitered about in front of my cell. Although the wall acts as a screen, which allows me to write these letters without their notice, it does not hide my face as I do what others are privileged to do in private. As I was sitting on the toilet behind the wall the two of them began to laugh and mock me. They started saluting and making rude noises as I was evacuating my bowels. Disrespectful bastards. Now that he has remembered who I am, I will have him exactly where I want him. I will place the photograph on the ledge close to the bars so that he will always have to look at it and remember that I am the Prime Minister.

I am exhausted. Between the lights, which never go out, and the bloody birds outside my window, I have not been able to sleep. I have complained to the guards but they tell me to take it up with General Zela.

Ferdinand

p.s. Please send my Bartlett's quotations and Oxford dictionary, which are on the shelf behind my desk in the study.

David,   22nd Jan

The channel for communication appears to be working. Your letter arrived with my breakfast this morning. The courier had slipped it inside the *masala dosai*. It was only after I had worked my way to the cumin potato filling, as I was tearing the crisp pancake around it to dip into the lentil sambar curry, that I discovered the crumbled, tightly folded paper. A clever touch on his part, I must say. I hardly expected such ingenuity from a Qalit. All this is to say that we may safely rely upon the cunning fellow from this juncture. You ask, "Surely, you do not hold me or SNN responsible for your incarceration?" Indeed, Sir, I do. You must know that your network's lengthy obsession with the political affairs of Chomumbhar single-handedly emboldened the National Front to plan and perpetrate the overthrow of my government. Because of you, the National Front is now the sitting government while I sit in this hellish place.

The Americans also betrayed me, despite the fact that I have been a staunch ally and loyal friend of the United States for more than thirty years. When they first came to me in the late 50s with their fears about Communism and their Domino Theory, I listened. They sent an idealistic young man spewing the theories of York Harding to give me lectures on democracy.

"If Indochina goes, Siam goes, Malaya goes, Indonesia goes, Chomumbhar goes," he told me.

"What does 'go' mean?" I asked him.

"It would be the end of your country," he said.

David,   25th Jan, 10 PM

Pyle and his superiors were so simplistic about everything, but Lady Lalitha insisted I deal with them. "They need Chomumbhar to host their military. We need a benevolent superpower as our protector." She told me to negotiate from strength. "Not so benevolent, my dear. Their foreign policy is driven solely by self-interest," I told her. Pyle bore that out by igniting a civil war in Indochina, funding insurgents to fight the French as well as the Communists. I never knew a man who had better motives for all the trouble he caused.

Nevertheless, I changed my mind about America after President Kennedy took office. The President and the First Lady bowled us over during a visit to Chomumbhar in 1962, and our relationship blossomed after that. I signed a lease for them to install a base in Riyalh soon after the visit; it was in our interest then to do so. However, twenty-five years later, as the lease was about to expire, I questioned having such a large American military presence in my country. It was no longer necessary. Communism was dead except in the mind of that Cuban imbecile, and our own economy was growing in a dynamic way. I gave the order for the military base to close, and the Americans went home. It was the beginning of all my problems. I will stop now, as the courier will be here any minute. I might as well put him to use.

David,   28th Jan

I find your broadcasts and analysis of the events in my country tedious, an extended torture; yet, I am never able to escape you. The television situated outside my cell is on at all times. It is strategically positioned out of my reach, so that I can never turn it off. My jailers have programmed it so that it receives only three channels: NFN bulletins on the quarter hour, your network, and BBC1. NFN is nothing more than a propaganda machine hastily assembled by the National Front to validate the coup. Zela's goal is to brainwash the citizens of Chomumbhar, while at the same time contributing to my psychological breakdown.

NFN's diatribes against everything I have accomplished for our nation over the last forty years, though cowardly, are not surprising. I myself used television and radio to educate the citizenry. However, I expect much more from the Western free press. BBC has been respectful in their coverage but your reporting has been atrocious. Day after day, you pronounce inflammatory, unsubstantiated statements about me and my leadership of Chomumbhar. I am disturbed that you and your network have allowed yourselves to be manipulated by my opponents in such an obvious way.

Ferdinand, my son,   29th Jan – 11.43 pm
   Yesterday, there was a fight in the yard. All because of bathing. The men here depend on routine to give shape and meaning to their days. They know, for instance, that Wednesday is shower day, a sacred routine that cuts the week in half. A new guard who started only this week told the men to get ready for showers yesterday—Tuesday, that is. They became quite violent and all but killed him; he was driven out of the gates in an ambulance. I stop now for no reason other than that it is raining.

Lalitha, my dearest,   30th Jan - 1.03 am
   It just rained—one bit of life in this horrid place. It had been so hot since I arrived here. I could smell the earth cooking in the sun and the waste putrefying in the rubbish dumpsters and communal latrines below. I felt very unclean, as they had not allowed me shower privileges, and the faucet of the washbasin only yields dribbles of water. It has been a terrible hardship for me not to have my good suits and my three daily showers. Finally, I took matters into my own hands: I gave one of the guards my college ring in exchange for an enamel basin, a bar of soap, a towel, a face cloth, toothpaste, and a toothbrush. Though they have reduced me to barbarism, I have tried to maintain my hygiene as best I can. As soon as it started raining I noticed that the ceiling of my cell leaked in several places. I placed three empty condensed milk cans, my enamel basin, and my enamel mug on the floor to catch the drips. I sat on the bed and watched the drops hit the wells. They made different noises: tingting against the enamel, dunkdunk against the aluminum, and when the containers filled a bit, there was a blublub noise. I stretched out my hand to the leak at the foot of my bed, cupped it, and caught the drips. It occurred to me that there was enough water to give myself a sponge bath, so I rubbed soap into my washcloth and moved from leak to leak around the room. A good solution to a pressing problem.

I will sleep easily tonight, dreaming of you, of rain, of our son, of this country that we built together.

Freedom, my love.

David, 30th Jan - 8 am

As I said earlier, we had a strong relationship with America for many years. America needed friends in the region. They had their hands full with Indochina and needed allies. President Kennedy knew he could count on me. There was history to be made, and we seized the opportunity. With America on our side, nothing was impossible.

Lady Lalitha and I had ambitions for our nation, and the U.S was essential to our plan for realizing them. We had to finance the entire range of infrastructure and programs a developing country needs. Lalitha wanted a national airline with a fleet of Douglas and Boeing jets. We needed an international airport, hangars, highways, financing for municipal buildings, and education programs. Lalitha wanted a national museum and a library.

When the US pushed hard to drop a military base with fifty thousand personnel in our midst, I worried. I knew what had happened in Italy and Korea. Whole villages saw that the way out of poverty was through hell, by servicing the military. However, my worries were always eased by timely and generous capital infusions from D.C. Our relationship with the US was a "win-win situation," as you Americans are fond of saying.

Lalitha, 1st Feb

What is the meaning of this? I count on you for thoughtful, encouraging letters and you send me, *The Encyclopedia of Birds*. What use is such leisure class rubbish to me? Some empathy from you would be a fine thing. I look forward to conduct that is more mindful from you. You will rue the day you disrespect me.

David,   1st Feb – 11 am

It was only with this 21st century leadership that everything changed. When the lease for the military base was about to expire, they began to make outrageous demands I could not meet: expansion of their base for eighty thousand military personnel; a nuclear power plant; a waiver on tariffs; and open markets for all their products. I put my foot down; I sent the forces packing.

"We don't need guns, we don't need gum, and we don't need fast food," I said. Some months later, the American ambassador sent me a letter expounding the benefits of selling our water rights to a company "that knows water." "Bechtel will own my island's water over my dead body," I told him.

I knew the special relationship was doomed when they began talks with General Zela and his party. Every day, the U.S Ambassador sent me dossiers about my government's violation of democratic principles and human rights. This was an aggressive act. "We are a free and sovereign nation answerable to no one," I told the Ambassador.

Soon after that the Americans decided it was time for regime change. The Secretary of Defense gave a press briefing in which he threatened me with a 21,000-pound bomb that would decimate my country. Zela thinks all his troubles are over, now that I am behind bars and he is installed in power. He does not realize whom he is dealing with. He will wake up one day and find that he has lost favor with the Americans, just as I have.

p.s .If you would be so kind, please send a carton of Dunhill Reds (I will not smoke anything else) via ordinary channels.

Ferdinad, my son,   3rd Feb

You must assume the sacred trust of saving our country. It is my hope that you will mature and grow wise from my suffering, so that you can be useful to Chomumbhar. In time, I expect you to plan the liberation of our island from Zela, and claim the mantle of leadership. Remain strong. Look after your mother. Fight the good fight.

Lalitha,   4th Feb
I had no idea we had such a variety of birds in our great country. I have a ledge outside my small window, which seems to be a sort of mecca for the creatures. I spotted a woodland dollar bird, which has a brown beak; the ash-colored drongo that is quite a show-off acrobat; the sunbird with an olive beak; and the black-napped oriole. When we take up office again, we must commission a bird park like the one Lee Kuan Yew built in Singapore.

David,   5th Feb
Your communiqué arrived safely, as did the cigarettes. Thank you, but do not think for one moment that you have redeemed yourself in my eyes. You persistently slander me and my leadership without knowing the facts. I surmise from your letter and your pointed interrogation of me, that you are infected with very rigid American notions of democracy. These views taint every subject you seek to analyze. Yesterday, you used your news segment to discuss my leadership style, which you deemed autocratic and insensitive to human rights. Your neglect of context is astounding. You failed to account for Chomumbhar's many complexities: that it is a Third World island nation with few natural resources save for pearls; and that it has a large and illiterate underclass cursed by poverty, drugged by religion, and shackled to useless tradition. Do you think Western style democracy and ruling by consensus would have accomplished anything for my people? Do you think the road to progress was easy for our little island? I am an engineer by training. I applied engineering principles to the problems that faced us so that Chomumbhar could rise to its true potential. However, experimentation can sometimes lead to unexpected results. I will confess that in getting to where we wanted to, we did make some mistakes, and perhaps committed one or two large-scale errors.

Lalitha, 7th Feb

I am deeply disappointed with our boy. I thought he would have planned an insurgency by now. He does not seem to have any vision or even ambition. His letters are hackneyed and uninspiring. He tells me he is taking care of things. What things? At his age, I was leading our country in battle against the British. Lalitha, where in this boy is there anything of me? I am six feet two inches tall, he is a five-footer; I am a dynamic leader, he is a philosopher with empty thoughts. Let it be said: the issue of my loins is an imbecile. Do you swear upon St. Francis, Lord Khrishna, the Buddha, and Prophet Mohammed that he is mine?

Lalitha, 8th Feb

Forgive me for questioning Ferdinand's paternity. He is such a hebetudinous dunderhead that it is beyond my imagination how he could be mine.

I had a vivid dream this morning that we were in our bedroom at the Palace, getting ready to go to a gala dinner at the Goethe Institute. You came to me looking more beautiful than I have ever seen you, wearing a bright red sari with silver embellishments. You asked me to help you put on your tiered necklace of pearls. I became irritated and frustrated as I fumbled with the tiny clasp of the necklace. When I tried to force the clasp open, the necklace broke and all the pearls scattered to the floor. You vanished, but I managed to save one of the pearls—a large, round, blush pink, a perfect nacreous marble. Before I opened my eyes this morning, I put my hand in the pocket of my prison jumpsuit, and there it was. I rolled it between my fingers like a prayer bead. Alas, it evaporated when I awoke.

David, 10th Feb

You declared in your last news broadcast that Lady Lalitha is an Eva Peron-like figure, widely feared and reviled. Since the

First Lady is under house arrest and cannot speak for herself, I must take up the cause of defending her. Lady Lalitha has been our nation's finest ambassador overseas, and the most caring advocate for the women and children of Chomumbhar. In four decades as First Lady, Lady Lalitha was the architect of many important policies and laws that improved the lives of our people. I ask you to look at the facts before you distribute these fictions about my administration to a watching world.

David,   14th Feb

How dare you continue to broadcast these outrageous falsehoods? Your assertions are so blatantly wicked that I dare say that if I were not incarcerated, I would have you and your production bureau rounded up, given your last meal and cigarette and shot. Your lack of respect for truth and accuracy has begun to inflict great damage on my reputation as an international statesman. Furthermore, the First Lady is living a nightmare because of your daily discourses. Lady Lalitha and Ferdinand Jr. are under round-the-clock surveillance, their every word and action monitored by armed guards of the National Front. Hooligans drive by the house at all hours of the day and hurl rocks and shout insults and expletives at my wife. Such disrespect, as if she were a commoner, as if she had not spent her life being a mother to us all. The callous disregard and lack of respect they show her is, in no small part, due to you. You have demonized her and made her a convenient effigy for the masses.

Lalitha,   15th Feb

The reason for the large bird population is the mangrove swamps and mudflats not too far fom Dalimar. I just saw a lesser adjutant. It was about 120 cm tall with a white body and dark grey wings. A proud fellow, despite the fact that he is bald; he reminded me of Soloman Ashani, the chief magistrate. Both have a superiority complex born out of an inferiority complex. When the guards are not around, I try to get a peek by climbing on the cot and hitching myself up by the bars so that I can get a good view of the ledge outside my window. I cannot hold myself up that way for long, but I have managed to see some wonder. A little flameback sparrow, beautifully plumed (ruby red on her cheeks, blue under the eyes) is building a nest. Such an industrious lady, each day she brings some new things, a few little twigs, some leaves, some long grass. Since her beak is so small, she must make many trips back and forth. Yesterday, just to show her how impressed I was by her perseverance, I left some chapati on the ledge. She liked it, I think.

David,   17th Feb

It has been said that Jonathan Swift was referring to journalists when he wrote about "the most odious and pernicious vermin that nature ever suffered to crawl upon this earth."

Ferdinand Jnr.,   17th Feb

If you are incapable of serving your country, I suggest that you give some thought to what you plan to do with your life. You seem to have little intellectual curiosity or interest in the world. Perhaps you are meant for commerce. True, I have called peddling a crude profession, but you seem especially suited to it. I had hoped that you would see that serving our country was the best and most worthy path you could follow. Since you have nothing to offer our country—no vision, no dreams—I implore you to set yourself up in the trades. I am sure you will find any number of businesses eager to welcome you simply because of your name. I urge you to get on with it.

David,   18th Feb

Your remarks about my governance are factually incorrect. May I remind you that I was elected eight terms into office?

They were all, without exception, landslide victories. Therefore, I cannot be, as you so crudely announced in your broadcast earlier this evening, "a perverse, megalomaniacal, morally confused dictator."

Lalitha,   20th Feb

My flameback needs to learn to be faster. The larger birds bully her, and her own slight body handicaps her. No matter how brave she becomes, she will never be able to assert herself. If she could just learn to be more cunning, she would be all right. When I leave chapati for her, instead of eating it right away, she saves it. It is, on the one hand, an admirable quality that she keeps an eye on the future, but on the other, she exasperates me. She refuses to face reality that the bigger birds pounce on the bread. I would like to see her defend her provisions.

David,   21st Feb

There were many people milling about near my cell today, as I had complained of chest pains since morning. The doctor arrived with two undersecretaries, one Permanent Secretary, Dr. Ayub Khan—the health minister bastard, a priest to confer last rites, and a phalanx of armed security guards brandishing Kalashnikovs. The reason for all the attention is not that they give a blasted, bloody damn about me, but that my death would be very damaging to them.

"We can't have you become a martyr now, can we?" said the Permanent Secretary.

"You've become something of a romantic figure among the peasantry," Ayub Khan said, wrapping a black cuff round my arm.

"Soon they'll make holy pictures of you," the Permanent Secretary smiled. "Enough of this screwing around," one of the undersecretaries said.

I glared at him, a walking digestive tract who presumed to

speak in my presence. He slunk into the corner with the other undersecretary. I was happy to see that despite all the madness, at least the order of the caste system was intact.

"If it was up to me I'd call for your execution, but General Zela is afraid the peasants will make you a saint." Dr. Khan pressed the stethoscope to my chest. Turning to the priest, he said, "The Prime Minister is going to burn in hell no matter what you do."

The priest looked at me, made a sign of the cross with his open palm, bowed his head, and left the cell. The doctor attributed my chest pains to stress and ordered bed rest. When I declared my rights under the Geneva Convention, he gave me some Tylenol.

Before this extraordinary public situation, our swift-thinking courier had been in the very act of passing me your latest missive. When the entourage came into my cell, the courier threw it in the toilet and shut the lid. After my visitors left, I fished the note out of the toilet but found I was unable to decipher your hieroglyphics. Please resend your last communiqué.

p.s. While I was serving my country these many years, I had no use for music or literature. However, I presently find myself with time on my hands and would welcome a cassette player and some recordings. Wagner, perhaps, or Strauss. This also seems as good a time as any to begin Dostoevsky and Shakespeare. You may send them anonymously through regular channels.

Lalitha, 23rd Feb

This morning I spotted a whole flock of brown shrike. They have heads that are either gray or brown or chestnut, and black bands on the sides, from ear to crown. Their foreheads and eyebrows are white. Some of them have black mottling on their faces and flanks. They are very far from home: migratory birds escaping winter in Manchuria and Japan. No wonder they are so quarrelsome and loud.

David,   25th Feb

I am in receipt of your package, which was in good order. I do not respect *Hamlet*, I shall therefore read *King Lear*.

I grow tired of these letters I must write you in order to set the record straight, yet I don't see that I have a choice. Yes, it is true that the opposition party consisted of no more than ten individuals at any one time. However, I think you will concede that if they had even remotely appealed to the masses they would have snatched victory from me honestly. Lacking appeal or ideas, they chose instead to wrestle leadership from me in an ignominious, illegal manner.

You and other Western journalists have failed me. You were negligent in addressing all aspects of the problems facing my island nation for the sake of simplifying the news. Brevity seemed to be your guide. Thanks to public opinion shaped and formed by you and others in the Western media, I am now faced with the very real possibility of lengthy imprisonment. I have learned that the National Front is planning to trump up more charges against me, including national plunder and crimes against humanity. If they prevail, I will probably be sentenced to life imprisonment at the maximum-security facility on Malim Island. Malim means "night" in our native tongue, and I think it is conceivable that night will soon fall upon me. I see now that I have no one I can trust except my wife and son, who can be of little use to me in my time of suffering.

Lalitha,   28th Feb

Each year 4 to 5 billion birds from all over the world migrate from north to south, and back again. Chomumbhar is a transit point for birds from all over the world. Fancy that! This morning I saw an Arctic tern and a milky stork. One comes from Farne Island, the other from Siberia. A voyage of over 15,000 miles—such a long journey! They remind me how far I myself am from home.

David,   2nd Mar

After giving your latest communiqué much consideration, I have decided to cease correspondence with you. The stakes are too low. This exchange has only a fifty- percent chance of educating you. Either you will see things from my point of view, or you will remain blissfully ignorant of the facts. However, the outcome for me, I am afraid, will be the same. I will remain in prison. Trying to enlighten someone with a limited capacity for understanding is mentally draining and physically exhausting. I do not wish to bother with you anymore, and ask that you cease communicating with me at once.

Lalitha,   6th Mar

Almost spring in the Northern Hemisphere. The birds will start getting ready to go home soon. They will spend all their time eating before their journey, often doubling their body weight. They will store enough fat so that they can fly non-stop for up to 90 hours! When the weather conditions are right, they will set off, sometimes flying 500 miles non-stop before touching ground. Because flapping wings uses up too much stored energy, the birds, especially the larger ones, will soar and glide as much as possible, using the winds and thermals to urge them forward. They will exploit the winds and thermals in order to limit their energy loss to half a gram of fat per hour. They are such daring, intelligent, strategic thinkers. Our idiot of a son could learn a great deal from them.

David,   11th Mar

Ignore my last missive. After sleeping on the matter I have decided, for the sake of future generations, to articulate my ideas and philosophies and explain myself to the world.

David,   16th Mar

Your letter reached me earlier this morning. I am open and equal to your challenge to expound my philosophies and actions for the sake of history. It is no small task, and I will have to set aside the very real anger and hatred I harbor towards you, so that I may begin to let the world know who I really am.

David,   20th Mar

The first thing you need to know about me, the most important thing you need to know about me, is that I have given my life to my country. I assumed the mantle of Prime Minister when I was just thirty years old. I had been educated in England and America, and had returned to Chomumbhar dazzled by what I had seen. It is common knowledge that for a time I, Prime Minister Ferdinand D'Souza, was ashamed of what Chomumbhar was not. I will not deny that I wanted my country to be like the countries to our right and far right. I wanted us to strive to be like Singapore and Japan, and ultimately, like the G-7 countries.

The things I saw during my official visits abroad, especially technology in all its applications, impressed me. What of it? Had not technology helped every Western country attain the golden ring of prosperity? I was not interested in the common application of technology for automation and mass destruction, for I was not interested in cheap manufacturing or building nuclear weapons. I was interested in technology that could be applied to the pressing problems that faced our nation. We had no large-scale agriculture of our own, although we had cottage cooperatives growing highland tea, roses, and many varieties of orchids. I wanted to use genetic and biological engineering to develop feasible food crops, especially our own rice, instead of importing Chinese rice. I wanted to explore the use of hydroponics and other such methods of agriculture. I was also very excited about the application of technology to address population issues.

Lalitha, 21ˢᵗ Mar

Though the swallows are ordinarily the quietest of the birds, they have been chattering non-stop, like people making plans. Perhaps they sense that summer is unfolding where they come from.

David, 25ᵗʰ Mar

Your package was appreciated. *Crime and Punishment* will certainly keep me engaged for several weeks. Regarding your request that I discuss my revolutionary ideas about population control: yes, why not? You have caught me in a good mood. I have just been fed a fantastic six-course Mawar meal because it is Independence Day. Zela was no doubt feeling guilty about keeping me, the Father of Chomumbhar, incarcerated in prison on this auspicious occasion. You may look up our history: if it were not for me, Chomumbhar would still be a British colony. My paramilitary defeated the English; my victory ended the last of their adventures in the East. In any case, I am in a good mood. The meal was a glorious one, a symphony for the senses. Each dish was prepared with ancient Raj spice formulations, and calibrated to tweak only a single taste bud at a time—one note at a time. Nevertheless, I must dwell on it no further. I must harden my heart to it so that I may never be addicted even to the idea of it.

First, I want to give you some sense of the size of my country's population problem. When you combine the main island of Chomumbhar and the ten smaller islands, we are only one-third the size of Australia. Yet our population in the early Eighties hovered at one hundred and sixty million people. These were alarming numbers. Obviously, when a bowl of rice is shared among more and more people, everyone's welfare is diminished and everyone is pulled down. You can see how overcrowding would be a problem that hung over our heads. I worried a lot about the problem. Those worries and concerns were the genesis of my Population Policy.

I remember that around the same time, I had to implement new burial laws for the country because we were running out of cemetery space. We mandated cremation. Those who refused cremation on religious grounds were informed that all ground burials would in future be vertical instead of horizontal. Many citizens were upset but I persisted. Burying people standing up saves space. It is an engineer's solution: elegant and efficient.

If you know my island's history—about the coming of the Jesuits and Saint Francis to our shores in the 16th century—you will realize why we are a pedagogical, rational, scientific people. The first Jesuits, including Ignatius Loyola and Francis Xavier, were noblemen and graduates of the Sorbonne. They were believers in knowledge, rationality, method, and competence; they were sympathetic to scientific study.

Lalitha,   7th Apr

A strange thing. Suddenly, I see large flocks of the Northern migrants instead of pairs and threesomes. Most of the great knot, the Eurasian curlew, and the gray-tailed tattler look plump; the brown shrikes are grotesquely obese. I have seen the birds swoop down across my window to the dumpsters and the mud groves in the distance, foraging for food. They have attacked the mangosteens on the tree in the compound as if it were their last supper. I saw a striated heron spear a mangosteen with its beak.

David,   15th Apr

Your report on Dateline SNN yesterday compelled me to write. I am troubled by the sensational tone of your story. You know nothing about the problems facing my nation. Your position that I had engaged in a campaign vaguely reminiscent of the killing fields of Cambodia is preposterous. Who told you that I admired Pol Pot? I followed his dealings out of intellectual curiosity, that is all. I am not a criminal, Sir. I am an educated man. I am a qualified electrical engineer. I took degrees from Leeds and Edinburgh before receiving my Ph.D. from MIT. I approach everything, including my personal difficulties, as engineering problems.

David,   18th Apr

I have learned that Zela's leadership council has decided to keep me here indefinitely, on charges that I am an enemy of the state. They will never execute me for fear that I will be bigger in death than in life. However, it is safe to assume that I will probably remain in Dalimar Prison as long as my natural life. Imprisonment robs the spirit first, then the mind, then the body. I am now nearing my seventh decade, and do not possess the stamina to endure this hell for very long.

I had imagined a different sort of retirement. I thought I'd be sitting in my study at Tilika Peak watching the sunset, nursing a Johnny Walker Black on ice, staring at the blinking cursor on the screen of my computer as I finished my memoir. I dreamt of contributing to the cultural canon, writing a profound thesis that would serve as a handbook for nation building. I am now cognizant of the fact that there will be no such book. I committed no crime and I did no wrong. Yet I have been chosen to pay for the sins of Zela, his followers, and my own citizens. I am Dimitri Karamazov, accused of a crime I did not commit. He shouldered the sins of history, the sins of his father, as well as the sins of the Russian people. But I hope to be saved like him, to see a meaning in my suffering.

Lalitha,   22nd Apr

My flameback is gone. In fact, all the Northern birds are gone except for the stragglers who are fattening up so they can join them. They left like thieves in the night. Such is the capricious nature of prison—anything that means something disappears without regret, ignoring attachments, shared history.

p.s. I am dispirited. I should like to release myself from the obligation of having to write to you so frequently. What is there left to say to each other?

David,   24th Apr
    It was indeed thoughtful of you to send me, of all things, Johnny Walker Black Label. In thinking it over, I realize that it would make a lot of sense for me to continue this correspondence for the express purpose of putting it into book form someday. There are several prison letters I admire: Nehru's, Martin Luther King's, even St. Paul's letters to his scattered followers. I envisage it as a last and final testament about my leadership of Chomumbhar. I give you agency to collate and publish these letters with only one stipulation: that the proceeds go to my wife. If you are agreeable to this, we may begin as quickly as you like, for there is much I would like to put down for posterity's sake.
    The power of my thinking deteriorates with each day in prison. Day after maddening day lived as if experience and feeling were severed at the knees. My body can take me nowhere. I miss seeing into the distance, my eyes can see no farther than twenty feet. My mind grows soft from probing the small things, the need to eat, to defecate, to sleep. My brain misses the complexity of life, the urgency of living, reason for being. If I do not engage in something important I will amount to nothing but waste. I must speak of big things.

David,   29th Apr
    The Zero and Right Population Growth Policy was my carefully constructed response to the population and demographic predictions that alarmed our statisticians. I knew we had to do something to reverse the numbers, and acted immediately to set up my Zero and Right Population

Growth initiatives. My right hand in this matter was Lady Lalitha. She shared my vision for Chomumbhar, you see; we saw an island paradise that could hold its head high among the world's nations, equal to Singapore and Japan. We recognized that it would become an impoverished nation if we did not engineer it for success. Therefore, we earmarked two hundred million dollars for the implementation of ZRPG initiatives through various means. We were able to secure monetary aid, including G-7 funds and U.S. pharmaceutical company grants, to address the problem.

We paired registered nurses with undergraduate economics students from the universities and sent them out, two by two, to every single neighborhood. Like apostles, when you think about it. The nurses educated the women about available family planning methods and distributed condoms and contraceptives. It was quite a challenge getting the Catholics to abandon the Vatican Roulette method they had been using, Rhythm or whatever they called it. Our findings showed that these methods were as effective as using perforated teabags. The Chinese and Indians kept having children, six and seven sometimes.

The economics students explained the financial benefits of having fewer children and told them about my government's bonuses to small families. I also immediately put into law the Solo Act, my one-child-per-family policy. The exceptions were university graduates. Ph.D. holders were allowed as many children as they liked. This is not elitism but practical common sense. The poor have nothing to give despite Mother Theresa's deifying of them. If I had been allowed to have my way without the international community hollering about human rights, I would have required anyone poor—laborers, pearl fishers, Qalit, and the like—to be sterilized and bear no children at all. Why burden the poor with unnecessary baggage?

David,   3rd May

The most visible expression of the ZRPG program was the creation of ultrasound clinics. The beauty of it was that we were able to establish clinics all over the island so that every village and hamlet in Chomumbhar had its own. To control costs, instead of using doctors and radiologists, we trained a corps of high school art students from vocational schools who had skills in photography. We chose only the most talented and intelligent ones, of course, and they became sonographers. We sent them for one month's training to India and China where they implemented ultrasound technology on a grand scale. Hiring the art students was a benefit to all sides. We did not have to employ radiologists or medical personnel who required professional scale salaries, and the young students achieved respected professional standing with relative ease. They became sonographers, instead of mere picture-takers.

p.s. The cigars you sent were rather good.

David,   6th May

In answer to your question: Yes, without a doubt, I was very impressed with ultrasound technology. I felt that it was an incredible new frontier in science for divining the future that offered a solution to our most crushing problem. It allowed us to invade the fetal space, a mystery through the ages, with the help of technology. By placing a transducer that broadcast high frequency sound waves—3.5 to 7.0 megahertz or million cycles per second—against the mother's abdomen, we could view everything inside the womb. Imagine! The ultrasound beams scanned the fetus, reflected back through the transducer, and recomposed what it scanned onto a video monitor. Fetal heart beat, gestational age, size, gender, growth in the fetus, malformations, and abnormalities, could all be accurately assessed from the images displayed on the screen.

We were very interested in the detection of abnormalities

in fetuses. You can understand, I hope, that for a country to develop to its full potential, we needed the brightest and the best. We could not afford to tolerate anything less than average. Therefore, abnormal fetuses were the very first class of fetus that we required terminated under our newly enacted Zero and Right Population Growth Law. In that first year of the initiative, we identified and terminated more than seven hundred abnormal fetuses. Imagine the heartache we saved those poor parents. They thanked our young sonographers as if they were gods. In fact, they were gods.

I should like very much to keep writing, but I am unwell. There is no air conditioning or even a fan in my cell. The air hangs thick and musty around me. In place of cleanliness, they throw pails of diluted Dettol over everything including walls and floors. The smell is offensive, my eyes are constantly burning and teary from it, and my headaches grow more frequent. I will post another letter when I am better.

David   11th May

Regarding the ZRPG Policy, Chomumbhar has traditionally been overpopulated with women. If you look at the figures until 1980, for every thousand boys born there were thirteen hundred girls. These figures were unacceptable to me as well as to my Party. We could see the dangers of having too many females, especially among the peasants. They were unable or unwilling to provide for girls because they were a bad investment. And who can blame them? Poor people who had daughters were screwed both ways. They had to pay dowry to get the girls off their hands and, worse, they could not count on daughters to look after them in old age, since tradition dictated that daughters entered their husband's family.

The situation as it stood was a catastrophe in the making. The burden on the poor was so great, so destructive, and we—correction: I, alone—found the solution. We determined that the second class of fetus to be aborted would be a controlled number of girl babies—ten percent. We wanted to bring down the gender gap in our demographics, and I can say that we had cooperation from all the expectant parents. The women understood that if they were going to be allowed one child, it had better bloody well be a boy who could bring in a dowry.

David,   18th May

The available technology had a ninety-eight percent rate of accuracy in determining the sex of the child by the twentieth week of pregnancy. Depending on the fetal position, you could see if it was a boy or a girl. If the fetal position was correct, we could see the testicles and penis on the video monitor. Seeing boy genitalia was always a cause for celebration. The mothers beamed and cried when they saw their sons' private parts. Everyone started calling boy genitalia, "crown jewels." With a girl, there would be three or four white lines, the labia of her clitoris. Our good man is here for a pick-up …

David,   20th May

We had carefully formulated protocols in place. Once the sonographers were certain they had seen either three or four lines, they had to fill out Form 77TXX, that is, the Second Class Fetus Termination Form. The sonographers had to sign the oath on the bottom of the form that they were one hundred percent sure that they had seen either three or four white lines. They absolutely had to see the lines to confirm that the fetus to be terminated was a girl. This was because the absence of the scrotum or penis did not rule out the possibility that the fetus was a boy. We wanted to be one hundred percent sure that we were not terminating healthy boy babies. Then the ZRPG Council, overseen by Lady Lalitha, reviewed the forms. Of course, not every case was selected for termination. The Council looked at all the factors—family income, education level of the parents and such. Money in the hand was honey in the lap as far as the council was concerned. In the western part of Chomumbhar and its archipelago that first year, out of four hundred abortions performed by the second trimester, two-thirds were Class Two—good numbers. The rest were the dregs I talked about earlier.

David,   25th May

You ask me about my moral and ethical judgments as they relate to my Zero and Right Growth Policy. You think like a woman. These sentimental questions are not valid when applied to a country like Chomumbhar. In our case, abortion has nothing to do with ethics, morals, religion, politics, or even a woman's right to choose, but everything to do with national welfare and good government. We should all agree on this without worrying about political correctness, human rights, and all that rubbish. Civilized and polite societies have accepted the legitimacy of abortion—this is an incontrovertible fact. Why, then, should we have mixed feelings over sex-selective abortion? And, why should we not use technology to help us in fetal-gender determination?

In all societies throughout history, the culling of females has been a widespread and accepted practice. In ancient Egypt, in Rome, in the Middle East, it was a common family planning method. Before ultrasound came along, women in India and China fed their newborn girl babies uncooked, unhulled grains of rice to choke them dead. Many gave them arsenic instead of first milk. Or suffocated them. Or drowned them. So why all this beating of the chest over fetal-gender determination and sex-selective termination? It is clean, responsible work performed in a clinical, medical setting.

This policy was well within the boundaries of my nation's conscience, our values, and our culture. It was the only method we had of keeping the population down. We were saving these parents a lot of heartache and grief and securing them a peaceful old age.

David,   28th May

The Zero and Right Population Growth Policy failed because of bureaucratic corruption on a grand scale. We found out, as the work progressed, when it was too late, that the sonographers were accepting bribes from anxious parents who did not want girls. The desire for boys is so ingrained in the culture that even when they could afford to keep girls, they opted out. The sonographers were doing an excellent business reclassifying Class Twos as Class Ones and manipulating the ten-percent quotas. If you look at the demographics over the last decade, you will see that the gender ratio is skewed to a troubling degree. When Lady Lalitha discovered the magnitude of the problem, we launched an investigation. The guilty parties were punished to the fullest extent of the law; they paid with their lives, I can tell you.

Of the marriageable-age citizens of Chomumbhar, you will see that there are only seven hundred women for every thousand men. Many of our men will not have women to marry. My own son, Ferdinand, has been unsuccessful in the marriage department because there is such a lack of girls. What I fear most is that men who are lacking women will turn to each other. I can tell you that we view homosexuality as a crime and will never condone it. It is an abomination. If we had set more stringent protocols for the three and four-line labia reading, our men would not be scrambling for wives now or making girly-girls out of each other. If I had just said, "Allow this one and that one to be girls," we would have had ratios we could easily live with. We would not have had to worry about our men having no women to marry. In that sense, the mission of the ZRPG was not accomplished. It is my single regret. I am deeply ashamed of my failure, that I did not manage the numbers more effectively. I remember Chairman Mao once saying, "Women hold up half the sky." I should have focused on pure math when we were implementing the program.

David, 30th May

You torment me with the most banal questions. Of course, I consider myself a good leader who served my people with distinction. I am certain that I will go down in history as the greatest Prime Minister and leader of Chomumbhar. I defy anyone to tell me otherwise. I have given my country everything that I had—my leadership, my intelligence, my vision, and my morals. In my thirty three years as Prime Minister, I promoted Chomumbhar's values, enhanced its position and place in the world, represented it overseas with honor, and increased its prosperity to near first world level. I have been a caring and compassionate leader who did everything within my power to make my country a progressive, prosperous, great nation. I wanted us to be nothing short of the very best.

Ferdinand D'Souza

Prime Minister,

Republic of Chomumbhar

A Sunday Affair

David Evans was at a loss as to what to wear that Sunday. If all his sources proved correct, it would be the day the US began its invasion of Chomumbhar to topple its leader, General Zela. For David and his peers, war correspondents from Western news outlets, the attack was long overdue.

Five weeks earlier, the major US and European media determined that a war was imminent, and dispatched their stable of political affairs correspondents to the sleepy, sleeping island on the Indian Ocean. Electronic and print journalists and radio personalities and photographers descended on the island to stake out a vantage point from which to observe and report the impending war. They were accompanied by retinues and baggage, the size of which depended on their celebrity. The highly paid, skillfully tanned, expensively coifed reporters from the networks arrived not only with large production crews, but impressive cargo—all manner of satellite-bouncing paraphernalia, microwave-resistant videophones and cameras (in case the winning faction tried to censor or jam outgoing broadcasts), bulletproof vests. Armored cars that could withstand most gun and missile fire were dispatched ahead of them from Detroit and Guttenberg.

SNN sent David with a three-man crew, standard equipment, and a lease on a soft -shell car. The group had waited patiently by the airport's rental car lane while the major networks breezed by them in their bulletproof SUVs. Finally, a cheerful yellow Passat with a relaxed island disposition pulled up near David and his crew. A black Hummer, impregnable and arrogant, slowed down in the lane next to theirs, and a window slid down like in *The Godfather* movie. "You're gonna get your ass blown off," the reigning Golden Boy of American network television mumbled, just like Marlon Brando, before speeding off.

"That wasn't very nice," Michael Reed, David's twenty-three year old cameraman said. Michael was a war virgin. He had told David on the flight over that he had rented *Saving Private Ryan* and *Three Kings* from Blockbuster to prepare himself. Cruising over Frankfurt, he had worried aloud that he might have forgotten to rewind the tapes. David, on the other hand, had been an embedded reporter for two weeks in Iraq. He had even completed a seminar on dressing bullet wounds and surviving as a hostage.

Irshard Sulaiman, David's sound engineer and second cameraman, was a Palestinian who had emigrated to the States as a teenager. Dressed in disco-era pants and poplin shirts and sporting a full beard and moustache, he looked like everyone's idea of a terrorist. David didn't understand why Irshard wouldn't help his own cause. Why not shave off the moustache and beard and wear a muscle shirt and khaki shorts?

Irshard was never to be seen without his earphones, an industrial pair with ear plates the size of small saucers and a wide connecting band. They either plugged his ears or curled around his neck like a boa. Irshad had once revealed, after David had plied him with several of his own insecurities, that he'd stayed alive in Gaza by running fast and pretending to be invisible. "If you're not there, the bullet won't reach you." Irshard had said. David knew what Irshard meant. He had been a morose, troublesome child himself. When his mother and teachers tried to reprimand him, he would close his eyes. If he couldn't see them, he felt he wasn't really there.

Completing the SNN team was Lisa Cohn, David's producer. She was the only seasoned war veteran among them. She had covered Rawanda, Somalia, Bosnia, Kosovo, and the first and second Iraq Wars. Lisa spoke seven languages, all of them with

American 'I can do whatever I put my mind to' self-confidence. She was the kind of ballsy female war correspondent Ernest Hemingway might have married; she even looked like Martha Gellhorn, the third Mrs. Hemingway, and wrote like Mary Welsh, the fourth Mrs. Hemingway.

David thought of her as an androgynous, post-modern chick—no breasts to speak of, no feminine wiles, and no sexual inhibitions. While covering the second Iraq war, Lisa had hopped from bed to bed with both men and women, one night with a reporter from *Le Monde*, another with a Greek anchor who looked like Arianna Huffington, and yet another time with a cameraman from Abu Dhabi. The press in Baghdad had joked that Lisa was on a humanitarian mission for the UN. At SNN, they called Lisa "The Ferret," because of her amazing ability to find tips, leads, sources, and stories. David hoped to bed Lisa before the war was through, despite the fact that he preferred blondes with big breasts, and mostly because the guy at *Le Monde* had told him that Lisa had pierced nipples and wore nipple rings.

For five weeks, the media corps had been staying at Chomumbhar's *Michelin* ranked hotel, *The Lisboa*. A few dozen of them had covered every major war since Vietnam. You could separate them from the neophytes like wheat from chaff. You knew they had seen a few things. You also knew they had given up the ghost on something quite fundamental—some necessary for the sake of sanity, God-holding mustard seed. There were also a few dozen war-hardened Australian, Canadian, French, and Japanese journalists who chased wars like tornado enthusiasts chased twisters. A handful of Swiss and Norwegian pacifists with *Reporters For Peace* said they were there to document the tragedy of war. They were treated like Untouchables—if their shadows fell on people, people walked away as if contaminated.

Then there were the happy campers like David, reporters who took dictation from the military, acted as if they were the

PR wing for the PR wing of the White House and the Pentagon, and still called themselves war correspondents. They liked war. David wondered why no one would admit the truth: that war is the only story worth telling, that it brings viewers home early from work, stops them from switching channels, and keeps them coming back for more. In war, there is drama, pathos, suffering, glory, courage, and death. There's also good and evil, good that turns evil, and evil that vanquishes good. The best part of war: there's no guilt, no one to blame. War is the greatest story. David was sure of it. It turned him on.

Everyone waited patiently for the first strike. In the mornings, the senior members of the press lay in beach chairs by the hotel pool, marinating in SPF 48 sun block. At noon, they showed up at the hotel's bistro to polish off the elegant buffet spread. At two, they recuperated with exfoliating facials and shiatsu massages. They ended the day by getting plastered to the gills and refining their karaoke skills at the hotel bar. Those who had covered the Gulf and Iraq wars couldn't believe their luck—that they were finally covering war in a country where booze was legal. They were also thrilled that the women were quite beautiful and didn't hide their bodies inside potato sacks.

While the correspondents spent most of their time at the hotel, waiting for the action to begin, their crews went out into the field looking for story leads. The assistants brought back nuggets of stories, which the correspondents then reworked and filed. They narrated feature segments on the history of the island and conducted street interviews about the imminent war. Half the population begged the American President to please mind his own bloody business, and the other half wanted to know if they could eat democracy.

The reporters broadcast human-interest stories about the US soldiers who were stationed on aircraft carriers on the Indian Ocean, and analyzed the arsenal of weapons and their powers of destruction. They read White House news releases and news briefs issued by the American Ambassador. The President said islanders deserved to sit down at the "buffet table of democracy." It didn't have quite the sex appeal or resonance of "Shock and Awe," but the media quickly christened the campaign, "Operation Buffet Table." David tried his best to come up with catchy leads: "islanders hungry for democracy," "guests at the table of democracy," "ravenous diners waiting for buffet," that sort of thing. In the interest of objectivity, the media interrogated the press secretary to General Zela, who pointed out that the US was hardly perfect. He said that Chomumbhar was perfectly capable of governing itself without outside interference.

The reporters also monitored the high stakes game of global diplomacy that might yet avert a war. Washington called General Zela a tyrant and blight on civilization. Zela called the President an imperialist and a lunatic. The President called Zela a threat to Democracy. Zela called the President a threat to humanity. The President demanded that Zela leave Chomumbhar within forty-eight hours. Zela told the US Ambassador who had delivered the President's message to go fuck his mother's pimp. War was inevitable. The reporters were pleased, aroused. They were turning soft from the rest, recreation, and debauchery. Their *Savvy Traveler* wrinkle-resistant pants were growing tight at the waist and crotch. Their extended foreplay needed a climax—a pyrotechnic-caliber, multiple-orgasmic, "I'm coming, I'm coming, I'm dying, I'm dead," climax.

Freshly showered, toweled, and deodorized, David Evans slid open the mirror door of the closet in his hotel room. His best all-weather blazer, water stained and limp from the previous day's monsoon rain, sagged from a hanger. His favorite chinos lay crumpled on the floor of the closet. The drawer below the television and above the mini bar—where he kept his laundered shirts, all of them blue—was empty. He had no clean socks. David dressed in his third best khakis, a clean enough white shirt that made his skin look blanched and fatigued, a tan bomber jacket, and socks pickled in yesterday's sweat. When he looked in the closet mirror he regretted his ensemble—it failed to pick up the blue of his eyes.

David's agent, Arthur Levy of Arthur Levy Talent Agency in New York, would be livid. He had usurped the role of mother in David's life ten years earlier, and had made David take a vow to wear only blue on camera. Arthur had successfully negotiated a $200,000 dollar raise for David two years ago on the strength of David's Q rating. David's Q rating, it needs to be said, increased twelve points among American female viewers aged 18 to 89 whenever he wore blue. Arthur, who had guided David's career all those years, made a point of calling David or sending him e-mail everyday. Arthur hurled his toxic bromides inspired by Sun Tzu's Art of War, across the ether and internet. That morning he had called David to say, "You're thirty-five years old, almost a has-been. There are young Turks right behind you from Medill and Missouri. If you don't show the camera that glint in your eye, you're going to end up back where you started."

David had shuddered at the thought. Ending up back where he started would mean the Food Channel, where Arthur had discovered him. David had been reviewing restaurants and blowing the lid off topics such as: garlic—nectar of the gods, secrets of a good tiramisu, and what else to do with chicken, when Arthur first spotted him.

"You've got a great face, and you've got an incredible voice. Cultivate a foreign correspondent's persona and I'll take you all the way to the top." Arthur had said.

Clearly. Arthur knew what he was doing. David was SNN's most popular political correspondent. After his stint in Iraq, he was assigned to head the news team at the network's bureau in New York. David was not an investigative reporter like so many of his peers, with their burnished J-school credentials who broke every story as if it were Watergate. The letters he had sent to Ferdinand D'Souza were ghostwritten by Lisa Cohn—the Ferret. However, David had no qualms about claiming the enterprise as his own. It had been the best work of his career, he told his peers. Lisa never corrected him. She was the producer—her work was meant to be invisible. David knew he was never going to be mentioned in the same breath as Edward R. Murrow, Seymour Hersh, and David Halberstam, but his blue eyes and voice were insured by Lloyds of London for two million dollars.

David rode the elevator down to the third floor, where the rest of the SNN crew were camped. He was irritated by his sartorial blunder, which would surely affect his Q rating, and his reeking socks. The door to Irshard's room was open. All three of his crew were there; they had requested adjoining rooms with connecting doors. David envied their communal inclinations, the ease with which they dealt with and tolerated each other. Once, David had begun to worry when some friendly bantering between Irshard and Lisa seemed ready to turn into a bitter argument. He heard the words "occupation" and "Zionism" over the tinkle of ice cubes hitting glass.

"Who was there first?" Irshard glared at Lisa.

"It's more complicated than that," Lisa said softly.

"It's ours from the river to the sea, it's not that complicated."

"Guys." David rose quickly. He hated confrontation. He preferred journalistic objectivity to moral positions. If the President of the United States had said that the sun rises in the West, David would report it without injecting his own opinion into the story. "President says sun rises in the West, some disagree," he might frame the story.

"I'm simply asking what she thinks," Irshard said.

"The whole thing sucks," Lisa said.

"That's a fucking copout," Irshard said.

Before David could make peace between them, Irshad slid

his earphones into place. Later, when David heard them having a lively discussion about the theme for an upcoming show, he was puzzled. Their anger, upfront and unconditional, ebbed and flowed like the moment-to-moment hurt of children.

Michael was sitting on one of the double beds arranging his equipment in the sponge cutouts of an organizer bag. In a war movie, Michael would be the character everyone would refer to as "The Kid." He would be the gentle innocent who humanized the cold, stern-jawed hero. His goodness would repair the friction between the hero and his command of bickering men. He would also be the first to die, because the world was never meant for anyone as innocent as that.

The Ferret was on her cell phone, talking in one of her seven languages. She was wearing cargo pants with pockets for everything and a skimpy white tank top. When she didn't hear what she wanted to hear, she muttered "piece of shit" in English and threw the phone on the bed.

Irshard was hunched at the desk over a laptop filing their latest canned segment.

"What are you doing?" David asked. Irshard didn't respond. "What's the deal?" David sat on the bed across from Michael.

Lisa grabbed an incoming fax from the machine, quickly scanned it and snorted.

"Listen to this," she said, waving it in the air. " 'More than a thousand bombs and missiles will be dropped over Chomumbar during the first strike. They are all precision-guided, deadly accurate, and designed to kill only the targets, not innocent civilians.' It's a joke and we're the clowns sent to tell it,' " Lisa said, as she stretched herself out on the chair. She raised her arms and laced her fingers on top of her head. Her tank top stretched tautly about her. Thick bushes of dark hair flashed from her armpits.

"Yeah, well," David said. He had no opinion.

"One of these days, David, you're going to have to

choose a side." Lisa said. The kindness with which she said it unsettled him.

"So what's the plan, boss?" Michael looked at David as he buffed his camera lens with the inside of his t-shirt.

"I think we should split up. Irshard and I will stake out the President's palace since everyone is guessing there will be an attack on Zela. You and Lisa take *Largo do Senado*," David said.

Lisa rolled her eyes. "If they're going to bomb Zela, do you think he'd be at the Palace? My bet's on him being at Senate Square. The tunnels in the basement lead to a bunker, I heard. That's where you should be. Michael and I will go to the palace, just in case."

"Yeah. Okay," David said dumbly, and slipped out of Irshard's room. He often felt like a fake; without Lisa, he knew he would be back where he started. He thought of Lisa's nipples, sure that he had seen the outline of the rings. He was sure he smelled raunchy. A war would make him feel so much better.

Two miles from *Largo do Senado*, David and Irshard heard the loud rumble of fighter planes. Immediately, air raid sirens started to wail. It was ninety minutes after the US deadline. Planes in formation circled below the cotton puff clouds, then rose up to hide under them; they looked cheerful, as if they were playing hide-and-seek. The sun streamed through the holes in the cotton puffs. David thought of the music he would choose to score the majestic sight, a John Williams overture from Star Wars, perhaps. When more planes joined the assembly below the cotton puffs, the rumble turned into a thunder and the sirens blared more urgently—with unremitting, ear-piercing shrieks that punctured the still air and curdled it. Birds, many thousands of them (sparrows, terns, herons, gulls, and many David didn't recognize) scattered in all directions across the sky. The others fell to earth like heavy dark rain. David knew some birds mated for life, and others reunited each year to make their spring and fall migration across ancient routes. He wondered if these scattered birds would somehow find each other again.

On the road ahead of them where the cars disappeared from view, they could see giant plumes of black smoke.

"I'm not ready to die." Irshard swerved the Passat off the road and onto a gravel path. David held on to the top of the window to brace himself, as the tires crunched over pebbles and grit. The dirt road ended near a phalanx of willows. Irshard drove into the curtain of willows so that long ropes and strands of leaves covered the windows of the car.

"We're not going to die." David stared ahead with determination.

"What, you feel it in your gut, do you?"

"It's not going to happen," David said.

"In the next life, I want to be born an American," Irshard muttered.

David shrugged. "I don't feel we'll die."

"As long as you feel it, then," Irshard said, as he reached in the back for his camera. He pulled himself out of the car, hitched the camera strap over his shoulder, and retrieved a large backpack and tripod from the trunk. He slipped the pack onto his back and held the tripod horizontally over the other shoulder.

Though David's hands were free, he did not offer to help. He followed Irshard onto the curve of a lane that took them to a row of elegant villas on a promontory overlooking Resurrection Beach and the Indian Ocean. They stopped in front of the first house and rang the bell. It was a Christian neighborhood judging from the statues of the Madonna and St. Francis Xavier on the lawns; everyone was bound to be at church. They walked up the lane and back again to the first house, and rang the bell again. The wrought iron gate was secured with an obese Chubb lock. "Smash it," Irshard said. David picked up a rock and hit the lock and the latch; it opened without protest. Irshard set his equipment down, tried the knob on the stained-glass front door, then followed the paved stone walkway to the back of the house. David put his hands in his pockets, puffed out his cheeks, and rocked back and forth on his heels.

"The barbarians are now inside the gate," Irshard opened the door from the other side of the stained glass. The house must have belonged to someone of account. It was filled with expensive furniture and rugs. A framed photograph of the President and his wife leaned on a rosewood chiffonier next to an alabaster statue of St. Francis Xavier and a marble Pietà. The books of Fernando Pessoa and Cesare Verde, the Bible, and *Lives of the Saints* lay on the coffee table.

The villa smelled of warm, bitter, nose-flaring odors of shrimps and prawns and octopus and spices. David and Irshard strolled into the kitchen. A colorful paella bubbled cheerfully in a crock-pot. Whoever owned the house had not left in a hurry. The kitchen sink was clean; the dining table was set for four. Several crystal and ceramic vases filled only with water stood on a table ready for flowers.

"I dunno," David said.

"Don't worry about it."

"What if these people complain? Breaking and entering?"

"Laws mean nothing," Irshard said.

"This is serious," David said.

"War has no memory, don't worry about it."

David followed Irshard up the stairs to a third-story balcony, which afforded them a panoramic view of the air strike. They could see B-2 stealth bombers and F-117 stealth fighters circling the skies. There was shelling and bombing in the distance. David counted 10 satellite-guided Tomahawk cruise missiles fired from warships out at sea. Irshard declared it perfect and set down his equipment. Irshard studied the view; he was forbidden by station rules to show war with context. An F-117 stealth fighter was always good on its own, out there in the sky looking like a giant erect penis. A bad image would be to show the F-117 ejaculating—dropping a 2,000 pound payload on a pearl fishery with a serene Indian Ocean in the background.

David leaned against the balcony railings and jotted down notes. He used his cell phone to talk to Lisa and his sources in the military. He was all nerves, his palms were sweaty; he felt too aware of the heat and the smell arising from his own body. He recalled an old woman he met at the island's central market the previous week, who had told him that there would be no war, that the Americans were bluffing.

"But why would you say that?" David had asked, incredulous.

"Saint Francis sees to it," she had replied.

"Snap out of it," Irshard scolded him, as he trained his lenses on David. "Too much shine on your face, lose it," Irshard commanded. David wiped a blotting tissue over his face, and waited for Irshard to count out the seconds taking him to "live." He delivered a three-minute "quick and dirty," announcing the launch of the war, and managed to answer follow-up questions from SNN's desk anchor in New York about the range of the missiles and the objective of the U.S mission. He did not mention Zela. David was secretly hoping that Zela would be killed or captured quickly before the US brought out the MOAB, the "massive ordinance air burst" bomb weighing in at 21,500 pounds. At some point on the balcony, they lost phone contact with Lisa and Michael. Over the next two hours, Irshad and David tried to put a lid on their boiling panic when their repeated calls to Lisa and Michael went unanswered. "I'm sure they're all right," David said, more to comfort himself than Irshard. "I guess," Irshard said, thankful that he could hide his worry behind the camera and his earphones. But David was filled with dread; he was certain that Lisa would have called him by then to brief him on the bunkers. They taped four three-minute live feeds for the prime time and late evening editions, and when they still hadn't heard from Lisa and Michael, David called the station chief in New York. As he waited for the SNN operator to patch him through, one hand cupping the phone, an index finger wedged in his other ear to drown out the noise of the planes, Irshard gestured for him to hang up. "It's not right," Irshard said into his own phone.

In David's final broadcast of the evening, he reported the news of his fallen crew. "Sources at Central Command and the field hospital on board the USS Liberty just confirmed the deaths of newswoman Lisa Cohn and cameraman Michael Reed, both of SNN. They were among one hundred and thirty people killed during combat operations at the Presidential Palace in Port Contadu."

By the time Irshard packed up his equipment, night had fallen. Howitzer multiple rocket launchers had stopped lighting the sky like fireworks, but Blackhawk helicopters without lights sliced through the inky sky like Friday night traffic.

David and Irshard drove in silence towards *The Lisboa*. David thought how brave it was of them to be so foolish. Irshard mourned the Gaza he was condemned to carry with him everywhere.

Memorare

My dolls were on the seat next to me. Omar, our chauffeur, was turning the dial on the radio to find something other than a humming sound. We were in the armored car that General Zela had assigned my grandfather, Rohan Rodriguez, the general's speechwriter. Omar had parked near Largo Dourado, the square at Change Alley. We were waiting for my mother and grandmother. I could see Mama and Nenah under the portico, haggling with the flower sellers. My mother tucked a bouquet of lilac orchids, with wine-colored spots wrapped in a cone of newspaper, in the back pocket of Nenah's wheelchair.

"Do you know about Missionary crabs?" Omar asked, as he looked at me through the rearview mirror of the limousine.

"Of course." I rolled my eyes.

I much preferred Daud, Omar's uncle, our former driver. But Daud had taken ill. After driving from Da Gama Drive to Resurrection Beach, from Port Contadu to Flore de la Mar, from Change Alley to Miramar, from Tilika Peak to Rua Domingo, for nearly three decades, Daud could not remember the road to anywhere. He forgot places, landmarks, directions, routes, things he had known better than the lines on his hands. Slowly, like a plant drying on the windowsill, first just dry, than cracked, then falling apart, Daud's mind took leave of him. But he was a burden to no one. He sat on a stool outside the servant's annex adjacent to my grandparents home, a soft smile on his face, happier than most people. His nephew made sure he was clean and clothed, and Sita pampered him with meals that kept him plump and his face unlined. He passed his days watching the traffic, fanning himself with a folded section of newspaper and watching the air stir in front of him. Omar took over Daud's duties, but he tried too hard, striking up conversations with me as if we were old friends.

"I will tell you anyway," Omar said. "Saint Francis Xavier and two other Brown Robes were sailing to Chomumbhar from Malacca when a furious storm broke out.

Saint Francis dipped his crucifix in the sea and the storm ceased, but the crucifix fell in the water."

"I know this story." Everybody knows this story; this fellow is getting on my nerves, I thought.

"After they landed, the crab dropped the crucifix in front of the Jesuits. Saint Francis blessed the crabs and the island. Which is why the crabs are called Missionary crabs and why they have crosses on their backs," Omar said. "And you can tell your friends that." He nodded at the dolls seated next to me.

My grandfather had bought them for my mother from Hong Kong, a long time ago. Asia, Africa, America, Australia, and Europe, because Antarctica was too long. Only Asia and America were left. Asia was missing an arm and a leg. America was missing both eyes—the taut, elastic mechanism that held the blue eyes in their sockets, snapped off years ago, and where her eyes were, there were now only two holes. America was also the place where my father, Ari Navidad, escaped to, after his disgrace. He had stolen a lot of money from the people, and Lady Lalitha, the former Prime Minister's wife discovered the theft. She wanted him sent to jail at once without a lengthy trial. But Grandpa Rohan appealed to the PM to spare Papa from jail. Because the Prime Minister held my grandfather in high regard (he gave the PM's words wings), a compromise was reached. My father would surrender his citizenship, leave the country, and never return to Chomumbhar for the rest of his life. Grandpa Rohan urged him to leave. "You need to go where people don't judge a man by his mistakes." My father agreed in the end.

"In America, I will make my fortune," he promised my mother, who had believed his promises for so long and then just ran out of belief. He wanted Mama and I to go with him.

"We can start again, the three of us, without roots, without baggage."

"All I have is my baggage. I would be lost without it," Mama said.

"You're my wife. I need you."

"You lie even now."

My father extended his hand to me. "Zara, wouldn't you like to live in New York? It's the best place in the world."

"She owns a piece of the sky here," my mother said, pulling me away from him.

My mother began the act of uncleaving herself from my father, with a petition to the church for the annulment of their marriage. She went with Grandma to see Father Daniel Sullivan, our parish priest. Father Daniel helped her fill out the preliminary investigation documents to be sent to the Tribunal at the Bishop's office. A month later, Father Daniel accompanied my mother and grandparents to the Tribunal hearing. Mama admitted under questioning that she had always known that my father would give her nothing but sorrow and take everything from her, but that she agreed to marry him anyway. The Bishop asked her if she hadn't mocked the holy sacrament of marriage by entering it so lightly. My mother denied it. When pressed to admit her error, she would not. "I made no mistake. One cannot hold back in order to love, it is best to do it without being stingy, to enter it blindly. And who is to say that we were not chosen simply to love Zara into being?"

Two witnesses had to swear upon the Father, Son, and Holy Ghost that my father had perpetrated acts against my mother in ways unbecoming of a Christian husband. The unholy acts included emotional, verbal, and psychological abuse, alcoholism, adultery, hedonism, narcissism, and spiritual and moral bankruptcy.

After the Court of First Instance sent the decree that freed

Mama from my father in the eyes of the church, she moved us both to my grandparents' house on Tilika Heights. There she reclaimed the bedroom of her childhood, and I took the room next to her. My grandparents were relieved. They had spent too much of their lives worrying about my mother and me. Grandpa Rohan had peddled his influence, squandered his money, and hatched elaborate plans to extract my wayward father from all his troubles. Nenah had mortified herself with pins and medals and prayed to the Madonna and Saint Francis for my father's conversion. Exhausted now, they were grateful that peace had returned to our lives. Sita marveled at the wisdom of everything. "No matter how far we go, we always come back to our beginning, isn't it?"

I was not a fearful child, but sometimes the empty space in my heart and mind that my father once occupied, and the life in front of me seemed so vast, so fathomless, that I would reel back in fear as if reacting to a slap, or hurl my dolls to the ground. Sometimes at night, I would stray into my mother's room and find her not there. She would be standing at the balcony past the French doors, staring at the carbon water lit here and there by the moon. "Mum?" I'd say. She would look at me with a troubled look in her eyes, and I would know she could offer me no comfort.

Now, so many years later, it was a surprise to everyone on the island, especially my family, that my father, who had gone to America vowing to become filthy rich, was being hailed as Chomumbhar's new leader. The Americans had decided to overthrow Zela and bring democracy to Chomumbhar. My father had been appointed by the Americans to become the new Prime Minister. The world media called my father, Chomumbhar's Leader in Exile.

"Exile!" my mother said. "He's a trinket peddler on a business visa!"

My father was all over television, saying things about

our island that nobody recognized. He said he was going to remake our country and bring us all "to the buffet table of democracy." "Buffet table of democracy! He's a bloody fool," Grandpa Rohan said. My father said he was going to bring us Freedom, Equality, Enlightenment, Peace, and Prosperity. He also promised other benefits: American investors, American oil and energy experts, and American water companies, who would sell us our own water.

"I thought God owned water. When did it become theirs to sell?" Nenah wanted to know.

"Zela will kill him," Grandpa said.

"Perhaps the Americans just want to keep Zela in line," Nenah said.

"They will come because they can," Mother replied. "Because my idiot husband has dazzled them all with his lies."

"It has nothing to do with us. God is on our side," Nenah said. "Francis Xavier will watch over us."

That morning, General Zela had sent for my grandfather right in the middle of the homily. Father Jean Perout's sermon was about faith in things unseen. It was very beautiful—St. Paul's letters to the Corinthians. But we were not moved, because we still did not know the man who had been sent from Belgium to replace Father Daniel. We could not wrap our tongues around his name. We tried saying his name the French way, but it was simply not natural for us. Parishioners called him Father Gene or Father J. Sometimes we called him "Peroot," which meant bellybutton in our language. Because he was a stern, unfriendly man, unlike Father Daniel who was a true islander, a true pearl, we did not care. We missed Father Daniel and wanted him back, but he had his own ideas.

"I have prayed very hard these many months," Father Daniel had said at his farewell Mass six months earlier. "When I was a young man, I was sure of so many things. I felt that in order to find God, I needed to sacrifice and surrender my whole life. For a time, God and the life of the church sustained me and everything seemed clear. But it was only with age that I grew less certain about everything. It was while I was cloaked in incredible darkness that I could understand my own weaknesses, my own willful nature. I realized that I could no longer love God exclusively and still love life."

We were sad for ourselves when we heard these things, but Father Daniel had found something he could not give up even for God. "I won't stop praying just because I leave the church. God is not locked in a gold box."

Change Alley was crowded that day. People were shopping for months instead of days. The traders looked pleased; nobody would bargain that day as everything was in demand. The merchants in the carpet and jewelry emporiums were less happy; people could only think at that moment of buying food: rice and beans, canned goods, things that would keep if the power died. The candle, battery, and kerosene sellers owned the day: they could set their own prices. Husbands and wives divided to conquer—they could cover more ground and buy more provisions if they shopped separately. Children old enough to make purchases were dispatched to buy the small things: bandages, rosaries, prayer cards, paper, pens. Younger ones sat dutifully on benches in order not to impede their parents' chores. Babies were carried in slings and backpacks, while rambunctious toddlers were strapped inside strollers and shopping carts.

From the car window, I could see Anan and Muni behind the counter of their stall. Anan was flipping chapati dough in the air. Holding the circle of dough by two edges, he whirled and whisked it in the air in a circle. The dough grew larger and larger, before Anan slapped it onto the counter. I saw Sita at a small table waiting for Muni to bring her order. She spent most of her Sundays at Change Alley sipping tea and scoffing cakes at Muni's stall, chewing betel leaves, visiting the merchants, and spending her money. When we saw Sita there at that hour, we turned away and did not acknowledge her out of respect for her privacy. We felt that she deserved to be left in peace on her day of rest. Father Daniel was sitting at a long table with benches facing Largo Dourado. A woman sat across from Father Daniel, her back turned to me. I could not see her face, only her long auburn hair, but from Father Daniel's face I could tell that she must have been very beautiful. Or else why would he look at her that way?

A young man wearing white swung his cricket bat in a large arc. A dog lying near him ran and hid under the bench, where Father Daniel and the woman with the auburn hair were sitting. The dog howled.

Anan yelled at the man with the cricket bat. "Hey! You! Go and do your cuckoo things somewhere else."

The young man flipped his bat over his shoulder like a rifle, flipped the other hand over a brow in a crooked salute, and walked stiffly in an exaggerated manner.

"Crazy fool," Anan twirled his forefinger near his temples, as he looked at Sita.

Li Li Loong sat at the table closest to the flower shop where Mama and Nenah were buying bouquets. My mother and Nenah called Li Li, "the woman with magic hands." Li Li Loong dressed all the women in my family. She had made my first communion dress, white with a pearl and iridescent beaded bodice, and a veil with blush pink pearls. Li Li was with Ng, the seamstress, who once had no words. Li Li was wearing a green batik tunic and jade green pants. Ng wore a sundress of mustard gold. They were eating noodles and talking. They must have had a lot to say to each other. They seemed to both be talking at the same time, finishing each other's sentences.

"I need to stretch my legs," Omar said, getting out of the car. He closed the door, and strolled to the center of the Square. He walked around the statue of St. Francis—once, twice, clockwise, then once, counter-clockwise.

The car lurched up in the air, its back tires still on the ground.

I bit the side of my cheek as it set itself down again. The glass in the windshield had cracked like a giant spider web, though it was still in one piece. Black dust settled over everything inside the car. I could feel it inside my eyelids stinging my eyes and clouding my vision, and in my mouth and nostrils. I spat out blood and saliva and dust, a thick paste like the henna women painted on their hair. I tried to make my eyes water, to wash the dust out of them. I blinked furiously to wipe away the grit. I looked out through the side window on the passenger side.

Everything around me was on fire. Great big plumes of grey and black smoke, gigantic conch shells, twisted and twirled in the wind. The people looked like black statues. Some burned like candles, others like joss sticks. Smoke rose from their hair, their bodies, and their limbs. Omar was slumped at the foot of St. Francis, his body twitching fast, then slower, until it stopped. Father Daniel was sprawled on the ground. The beautiful woman, who was ugly now, was crouched next to him, screaming. She was holding a severed arm in her hands. She was trying to attach it to Father Daniel's shoulder. Blood spurted out from the hole in his shoulder, like water from a fire hydrant. When the blood stopped gushing, the woman tried to press the arm into the shoulder. She sat back on her haunches, and rocked back and forth, holding the arm like a baby. Her auburn hair fell in a cracked veil around her.

The man with the cricket bat hit a metal ball that fell from the sky. Muni, at whose feet the ball exploded, shattered like a glass vase. The left side of her body flew back, and up, onto a balcony on the second floor. The right side stayed where it was; it had nowhere else to go. Smaller bomblets and cluster bombs exploded in the man's face like fireworks.

Ng lay on the ground like a broken toy. The back of her head was on the same side as her breasts. Li Li Loong looked like she was sitting on the ground, but her body from the waist down, was on the hood of our car. The jade green pants hung off her legs in rags, shredded like thick noodles. Judge Solomon Ashani was in four pieces, his bowels were outside of him. The dog, bloody, three-legged, but still alive, stopped whimpering and howling long enough to eat the judge's entrails. Nenah's wheelchair lay on its side, the top wheel was spinning round and round. Nearby, my mother and my grandmother lay charred, stilled, their bodies curled close together, in a question.

* * *

No grass grows over my dead. No mounds of earth cover them. No stems of marigolds, chrysanthemums, and white lilies perfume their final beds. They are buried in the Indian Ocean, at latitude 28 degrees south, longitude 78 degrees east, and in the vaults of my closed eyelids, and the reliquary of my brain, and the sepulcher of my heart, and the ossuary of my veins.

There is nothing left of my sleepy, sleeping island now. Chomumbhar is uncharted, ungraphed, undeclared, unseen on the atlases and maps and globes of this new century.

Still, I remember the colors of home, the orchids of twenty different purples, bougainvillea in two notes of red, blush pink roses from Gelinta Highlands, the dew still weeping off them. I remember the blue-green waters of the Indian Ocean, the sunlight shimmering on its surface like flitting, fluttering butterflies. I remember frothy sea foam rushing to shore like armies of galloping white horses. I remember Missionary crabs running for cover under the rocks on Resurrection Beach, the crosses on their backs reflecting two o'clock sun. I remember time standing still, and life traveling around it in circles and returning me to the same place. And I remember the blueness of a particular sky.

* * *

This is the patent age of new inventions
For killing bodies, and for saving souls,
All propagated with the best intentions.

--Byron

LaVergne, TN USA
28 February 2010
174455LV00002B/27/A